T0380712

BOUNDLESS GRACE

Grace in the Wilderness Series

BOOK 1

C. SHELL LEE

WESTBOW
PRESS®
A DIVISION OF THOMAS NELSON
& ZONDERVAN

This is a work of fiction. All of the characters, names, incidents, organizations, and dialogue in this novel are either the products of the author's imagination or are used fictitiously.

WestBow Press books may be ordered through booksellers or by contacting:

WestBow Press
A Division of Thomas Nelson & Zondervan
1663 Liberty Drive
Bloomington, IN 47403
www.westbowpress.com
844-714-3454

Scripture quotations are taken from the New King James Version. Copyright © 1982 by Thomas Nelson, Inc. Used by permission. All rights reserved.

ISBN: 979-8-3850-2714-9 (sc)
ISBN: 979-8-3850-2715-6 (hc)
ISBN: 979-8-3850-2716-3 (e)

Library of Congress Control Number: 2024911804

Print information available on the last page.

WestBow Press rev. date: 02/10/2025

CONTENTS

As the festive lights of Graceville twinkled in the crisp winter air, the town's residents reveled in the joy of Daniel and Emma's engagement. The Turner Inn buzzed with excitement, laughter echoing through its halls. Yet, in the midst of this joyous celebration, another story was beginning to unfold, one that would bring new faces and challenges to their beloved town.

Far away in the heart of the bustling city, Izzy sat in her sleek, modern apartment, staring blankly at the skyline. The city's vibrancy, which once invigorated her, now felt cold and distant. Her life, filled with material success and social acclaim, had grown hollow. She sighed, her heart heavy with an emptiness she couldn't quite understand. Just as despair began to creep in, her phone buzzed with a message. It was from Olivia, a name she hadn't expected to see. Olivia's words were warm and inviting, offering a break from the city and a chance to visit the quaint town of Graceville. The invitation was unexpected, and something about it tugged at Izzy's weary heart. On an impulse, she accepted, longing for an escape, even if just for a little while.

Her confident façade now had holes not visible to onlookers and her polished exterior seemed to be fading as she delved into the mysteries and truths within the Bible. She found herself wondering if she really knew who she was and if anyone else out there would ever care enough to peel back the layers and discover the real person beneath.

As winter melted into spring, Izzy arrived in Graceville, her heart guarded yet curious. The town's charm and the warm welcome from Olivia and the others were both comforting and disconcerting. She wasn't used to such genuine kindness.

One evening, as the sun set over the picturesque town, Izzy found herself wandering towards the Turner Inn's garden. There, among the budding flowers and the scent of fresh earth, she felt a glimmer of something real and hopeful.

Would Graceville's serene beauty and its kind-hearted residents help Izzy find the peace and purpose she had been searching for? And could she ever unlock a future she had never dared to dream of? Was there someone out there just for her?

As the days grew longer and the town prepared for another season of warmth and growth, Graceville held its breath, ready to embrace another soul seeking redemption and love. Would the magic of Graceville continue to weave its spell?

CHAPTER 1

HOMECOMING

Emma fiddled with the dials on her car radio, having lost the signal after rounding yet another curve in this beautiful yet remote valley. It was good to be home, but the lack of cell towers in the area could prove to be a problem.

When she'd left ten years prior, embarking on a career as a brand-new architect, she'd thought more about driving toward her big-city dreams than driving away from the place she'd called home for twenty-two years. Now that she was back, a wave of nostalgia hit her quite unexpectedly.

She felt like George Bailey in *It's a Wonderful Life* as he runs through the town after getting a second chance. "Hello, Graceville Public Library," she whispered to herself as she drove down the main street. She and her sister, Olivia, had spent countless hours there after school, each studying their respective passions. Emma had become an architect while Olivia became a journalist.

Next, she drove past the Main Street Diner. Memories of breakfasts with the family and root beer floats after the football games came to mind. Her stomach growled, reminding her she'd been driving for quite some time and should get something to eat. Miss Pat had been the waitress there as long as she could remember, but ten years on, she had probably retired by now. That would have to wait though, as she was expected at home.

As Emma continued driving through town, passing the drugstore and old-fashioned movie theater, now the community actor's guild, her thoughts went back to the day she had left for her "great adventure" as her father, Reverend Samuel Turner, had called it.

He and Olivia were standing outside their family's historic bed and breakfast, Turner Inn, as she headed for the city with her few worldly possessions. It was a beautifully sunny day, which she thought was a good omen. Reverend Sam's arm was around Olivia's shoulder, smiles of hope and encouragement on both their faces.

They waved goodbye – she didn't know how long they'd stood there, because her eyes were focused only on the future. She didn't see the tears in her father's eyes as she drove away.

—◊◊—

Thoughts of her previous beaux in Graceville came to mind. They had been scarce; after all, her father was a man of God, so the boys knew there'd be no hanky-panky.

She'd had no mother figure growing up, just her dad trying to fill both roles. Her mother, Barbara, had died of cancer when Olivia was about five years old. It came on so suddenly and she was gone so quickly…they were still researching wheelchair ramps, expecting chemotherapy treatments and suddenly, they were planning the funeral.

Emma was unprepared for that side of things when she reached the city. She was an excellent architect, but sort of a country bumpkin when it came to romance. All she knew came from the fairy tales where the prince or the knight sweeps the maiden off her feet and they live happily ever after.

That's probably why she'd fallen for Byron Monroe. He was slick all right. There was no hint he was actually the bad guy in the fairy tales. Attractive and charming, he'd eventually broken her heart.

It had taken her a couple years of online therapy to face the fact that his excuses for not keeping a job were nothing more than narcissism. Every time he quit – probably right before being fired – it was because he was "too good" for the job.

He was using her as what was commonly known as "arm candy" but she couldn't see it. A pretty, pleasant girl with good manners. People complimented him on his choice of female companionship, and that played into his self-centeredness.

His behavior toward her became more and more controlling, going from suggesting outfits and offering makeup tips to actually booking hair appointments to make sure she got it done the way he wanted. When she ended up with a short poodle perm, she'd finally had enough.

She looked at herself in the rearview mirror, her hair now long and straight, the way she liked it. *Never again,* she thought.

—⁂—

Emma was so close to home, but needed to stop for gas. She pulled into Gus's Service Stop and almost chuckled at the old-fashioned fuel pumps. They still had the old metal numbered tabs that flipped over to show the price of the gas pumped. No LED lights, and certainly no touchless payment option.

She started to get out of her car to pay the cashier when an elderly man in white-ish overalls bustled out of the garage bay up to her car. "Fill 'er up, miss?"

A bit shocked and thinking she was in a *Back to the Future* movie, she was momentarily speechless. "Mr. Gus?" she asked, trying to keep the shock from her voice. He was still alive and kicking all right!

"Yes...why, if it isn't Emma Turner. You're a sight for sore eyes! What brings you back to town? How is the big city? Does your father know you're here? Are you still drawing houses?"

Gus Williams was always so full of questions. He listened to everyone's answers, but never engaged in gossip. He figured people needed someone to talk to besides the reverend, who was a very good friend of his, and felt he was sort of a layman's confessor.

"Let's see, yes, my father knows I'm coming. The big city is...big. I'm back to town for a little break from all the hustle and bustle. I'll still be working, but a bit closer to home, for now."

Gus knew exactly what she meant. He knew the Turner Inn was in dire straits, just like so many other small businesses. There wasn't much to draw people to Graceville for tourism since the pandemic, so the Turners' bed and breakfast had been mostly empty for months.

"Well, hon, with you back in town helping your dad, I'm sure things will get turned around right quick."

She smiled warmly at him. He gave her a quick wink and started pumping gas as she walked into the store to pay.

CHAPTER 2

AN UNEXPECTED ENCOUNTER

Emma stood in the doorway to her dad's home office, aghast at the sight before her. On the desk, surrounded by papers strewn about and sticky notes everywhere, was a behemoth of a computer monitor. White, yellow, and black wires were stretched and twirled everywhere like someone had spilled a giant bowl of electrical cord spaghetti.

On the floor to the left sat an old computer hard drive tower, a yellowed printer sitting precariously on top of it, the paper jam light flashing a lonely signal to anyone that might help.

"Um, Dad, is this what you've been using for a reservation system?"

Reverend Samuel Turner chuckled from behind her. "Yes, Emma. And before you start lecturing me on keeping up with the times, remember that I'm not exactly a computer wiz. When your mom and I took over running the B and B from Grandpa, this was state-of-the-art technology."

Emma resisted the urge to shake her head. When she was younger, the Turner Inn Bed and Breakfast had been a pretty lively place. Grandma Turner would get up before the crack of dawn to start baking and making breakfast while Grandpa walked the dogs and tried to mend the chicken wire that was supposed to keep the rabbits out of the backyard garden.

The people who visited were often singles, writers or nature lovers trying to get away from it all. Occasionally they'd get a honeymoon couple or retirees on their way somewhere else.

Emma made her way into the office and sat down at the desk. "Okay, give it to me straight. You mentioned in your phone call that things weren't going so well. How many reservations do you have coming up next weekend?"

The reverend scratched the back of his head in thought. "Well, actually... we don't have any. But it is school vacation week, so people are all about the kids right now. Plus, the weather hasn't been so good—"

Emma turned to look at him. He was almost squirming with guilt. She gave him a forced smile. "It's all right, Dad. I'm here to help. I'm sure it's nothing you've done, it's just the world today. We'll fix it, you and I together."

"Actually, there's good news on that front," Reverend Sam said with relief. "Olivia will be home next week. She worked it out that she can do W-F-H for the magazine, or something like that."

"Work from home? That's great! There's one good thing that came out of the pandemic." Emma smiled a real smile this time. It seemed the universe was bringing the family together for some reason. And the way things stood with careers and maybe someday she and Olivia having families of their own, this might be the last time they'd all be together just the three of them.

That happy thought quickly turned into a sad one as she remembered her hopes for marriage and a family with "that rat" Byron Monroe. She hadn't gone into much detail with her dad about the situation, but she had spilled her guts to Olivia, who subsequently gave Emma's ex-boyfriend the moniker "that rat."

She shook it off. After all, like the Bible says in Romans 8:28: "We know that all things work together for good to those who love God, to those who are the called according to *His* purpose."

—⁂—

The first thing Emma did after lunch was move the computer and printer to a shelf and bring her laptop to the office. There was no wireless modem or router in the house, so she'd have to use her phone hotspot.

After walking around the house and grounds, Emma found a window ledge facing an unseen internet signal that gave her two bars, just enough to get up and running, but she'd have to make other arrangements to work on the B&B's website.

Her dad had to go to the rectory for some church business, which gave her a chance to look through the sticky notes and pieces of paper lying about. The majority of these were old reminders to pay bills or send notes and cards to past guests. One said to buy stamps. He was sending out actual paper notes, not emails? *Dad sure is giving it the old college try.*

Emma started a to-do list on her laptop.

First, view guest rooms to see if they need updating. Her grandmother had sewn many of the quilts and crocheted afghans in the rooms, which gave the place a cozy, homey feel. But Grandma had been gone for at least fifteen years now, so a refreshing uplift was inevitable.

Next, put all the guest information into a spreadsheet to track correspondence and reservations. She knew there was no way they could currently afford a real reservation system, so good old MS Office would have to do for now.

Next, a newsletter would have to be created but she had already mentally assigned that task to her sister, Olivia. She was the journalist in the family, after all.

Before embarking on any kind of marketing plan, Emma needed to make sure they could accommodate guests with, quite simply, what they were advertising…. beds and breakfasts. That meant food vendors and possibly a cook and housekeeper needed to be researched. The budget would of course dictate if the new hires were even possible. In the meantime, she and Olivia would cook and clean. In fact, she needed to go into town for supplies this afternoon for her and her dad.

She saved the document on her laptop and leaned back to look out the window. The view, even in February, was so relaxing. There were enough fir trees mixed in with the leafless oaks that the mountains were still fairly green. This was vastly different than her view from her office in the city. There, she looked out and just saw the building opposite.

As Emma peered out the inn's window, the architect in her noticed that the wood-framed glass in the window had that wavy look that only leaded glass can give. This old house had been built by her great-great-grandfather when he'd moved here to escape the city, just like most of the townsfolk.

She imagined what it had been like back then, with horses and carriages instead of cars and busses. Most of the town's architecture was Victorian, or at least Victorian-inspired. No McMansions, no housing projects. There was a perfect balance to the influx of just enough new residents to keep the town from growing stale, and therefore keeping the vibe flowing and adding a certain mystique to Graceville. Unlike many small towns, the locals did not shun the new people. They'd be a bit wary at first, gleaning information through conversation, but once vetted by the matriarchs of the town, "newbies" were welcomed.

—m—

After Emma and her dad enjoyed a simple ham and beans dinner, they sat down to delve into a more serious discussion of the issues the inn was having.

"Dad, I took a glance at the books today while I was setting up my laptop in the office. They don't seem to be really…complete," she began.

"No, I admit, I have been having trouble keeping up with things. I didn't want to ask Dot to be my assistant at the church and here as well. Best to keep personal business separate," he replied.

"That's true, and good thinking." Emma remembered Dot as being efficient at the church in keeping Reverend Sam on time to his appointments and getting the bulletin out on time every week.

Sometimes she was a bit sharp, and a few of the parishioners had complained, but Dot believed in God with her whole heart and wanted to please him, so she embarked on a mission to curb her curtness and be more helpful. She still was not the happiest and most pleasant person in the world, but everyone agreed Dot's efforts showed that she was trying, and no one could fault her for that.

"Since there hasn't been much business, it shouldn't be a problem, Dad. Not to worry." That was a phrase her mom had always used. *I guess it is true that we all eventually turn into our mothers,* she thought with a chuckle. In her case, it was a good thing, as her mother had been an amazing woman.

"Oh, speaking of business, we got a reservation request today. A man named"—Reverend Sam fished through his pockets and pulled out a crinkled sticky note—"Daniel Reynolds. Called while you were out shopping and said he's a struggling artist and needs to find someplace quiet to get some inspiration. I told him we would give him a winter discount."

"Dad, that's very kind of you, but we're trying to get the inn back on its feet, remember? Maybe let's not give any more discounts until we talk about it more and make it part of the marketing plan."

"Okay, boss," Reverend Sam raised an eyebrow. Emma blushed a bit. She respected her father immensely and did not want to dishonor him.

"Sorry, Daddy." She knew all would be forgiven.

—⚬—

A blue BMW pulled into the drive and Emma looked up from her laptop, the crunching of the gravel under the tires gaining her attention.

Out stepped a handsome man about her age. He stood up, stretched, and looked around, seeming to nod in approval. Popping the trunk and reaching in, he pulled out what looked to be a fairly expensive luggage set. *Struggling artist, huh?*

She made her way to the front door as he was climbing the porch steps and waited for him to ring the bell, as opening the door before then might have startled him.

Once he rang and the door was opened, she smiled and said, "Welcome to Turner Inn. You must be Mr. Reynolds."

"Yes, I made a reservation over the phone."

"Please come in and I'll show you to your room."

He stopped to sign the guest book, setting down his luggage and picking up the pen. Emma noticed his hands were...lovely? Is that the right word to use for a man's hands? She was drawn to the contours within them, they were smooth, and graceful as he wrote his name. Perhaps he really *was* a struggling artist, or at least an artist.

She felt a little self-conscious as he followed her up the stairs to his room. She had rented him the room at the top of the stairs to the right, overlooking the back garden, which was now closed for the winter. There were tasteful lawn ornaments and pea stone paths scattered about the garden, but more importantly, this room was the least squeaky and outdated of all their rooms at the moment.

Emma noticed a slight nervousness in his presence that made her want to chatter to fill the silence. "So, my dad says you're an artist. What is your medium?"

"Mostly oils, but I will probably just be doing charcoal or pencil sketching here. It depends on how long I stay."

Hmm, so he might extend his reservation...

She opened the door and ushered him into the room. Luckily, it was sunny, so the room looked especially bright and cheery. "I hope this will suffice," she said as she pointed to the bed, view, and bathroom door.

"Yes, this is fine, thank you. Do you know where I might grab a bite to eat later?" he asked as he set down his bag and turned to face her.

My, he is tall. Emma composed herself. "Yes, the Main Street Diner is open until eight p.m. After that, they pretty much roll up the sidewalks here."

He grinned. "That is exactly what I'm here for. Peace and quiet."

Emma wasn't sure if that was a conversation opener or a hint to skedaddle. *Skedaddle? I've only been in town a few days and already I'm picking up their dialect...*

"Very good," she managed to say. "Breakfast will be from seven to nine, we eat in the main dining room down the stairs to the left." She hesitated. Should she admit he was the only guest? It might make them look kind of lame. She decided honesty is the best policy.

"Since you are the only guest currently registered, do you have a preference of coffee or tea in the morning?"

He didn't even hesitate. "Coffee, please." Knowing the pandemic had closed many small businesses like this one and judging by the clean but outdated furnishings and creaking floors, he figured they were having their fair share of problems too.

"I'm glad I'm your only guest at the moment," he said with another smile to ease her apparent nervousness. "I did not expect many others at this time of year anyway, so this is perfect."

CHAPTER 3

THE OLD INN

The smell of blueberry muffins wafted through the ground floor of the Turner Inn and made its way up the stairs. The first door on the right opened and out stepped the inn's sole guest, artist Daniel Reynolds. The smell of fresh-brewed coffee along with the muffins made his eyes open wider. It was exactly seven o'clock but he figured they were ready for him, judging by the smell of things.

He followed his nose down the stairs and to the left. The pocket doors to the dining room stood open and the ambience was welcoming. Muted sunshine came in through the lace window coverings, highlighting the antique décor. Just enough knickknacks to make it homey but not cluttered.

Along the top of the mahogany sideboard were plates, cups and saucers, and utensils, set out buffet-style. A glass cake pedestal in the center held one of the objects of the aromas – fresh-baked blueberry muffins. Displayed around it was a nice board of cold meats, cheese, and fruit. But the coffee was nowhere in sight.

Just then, the door at the back of the dining room swung open and in walked Emma, backwards, hands filled with a tray containing a porcelain coffee pot with matching sugar bowl and creamer. She turned around and was startled at the sight of a man at the other end of the room.

"Oh!"

One hand instinctively raised up, causing the tray to list dangerously to the side. Daniel lunged forward in an attempt to assist but that only startled Emma further and she automatically backed up to retreat through the doorway. Unfortunately, the swinging door had swung to its rebound swing and had just returned, knocking her soundly on her backside.

At this she lurched forward, coffee tray now listing in the other direction as Daniel made a heroic effort to help avoid the impending catastrophe his presence had obviously instigated, arms outstretched like he was saving a baby falling out a window, completely focused on the tray.

As Emma fell forward and Daniel closed the distance between them, his hands leveled the tray and stopped her forward momentum. They made eye contact and froze in that instant.

The near-calamity turned into hilarity as Reverend Sam burst out laughing. "You two should go on the stage that was incredible! Better than Hope and Crosby."

Emma blushed and Daniel let out a breath he didn't know he was holding. "You okay?" he asked.

"I...I..." Emma burst into nervous laughter herself. "Yes, I'm fine, thanks. I was just surprised to see you down here so early..." Her eyes flicked to the clock on the mantel. It was 7:05 a.m. He wasn't early, she was a few minutes late.

He stood up and let go of the tray a little, making sure she had it under control. She did. "I couldn't resist, the muffins smelled so good –"

"No, you're actually right on time. I promise your breakfast tomorrow will be less...athletic."

Daniel started laughing, and now she laughed along with him. He had put her at ease in an instant. *Byron would have berated me for being a klutz.*

She had to get her ex-boyfriend out of her mind. Maybe she'd try some online therapy, or maybe the church in the next town would have a lay minister who could help. She would be too uptight to go to anyone in town. After all, she was the reverend's daughter. She didn't want to start any gossip that might affect his good work at the church.

Bringing herself back to the present quickly, she set the tray on the table. "Dad, if you're ready for some breakfast, come on in from the doorway and help yourself."

"Thanks, Emma. I'm glad this young man helped save Grandma's china coffee service. You must be Daniel Reynolds," the reverend said turning to Daniel and holding out his hand.

Daniel shook Sam's hand and smiled. "Yes, sir, I checked in last night. I grabbed a quick meal in town just before they closed and came back here and fell straight to sleep. Sorry I missed you."

"No worries, son. Last night was Bible study night at the church where I preach. I didn't get home until around nine p.m., which is very late around here. But if you can stand to stay up that late, you're more than welcome to attend. Interestingly, we're studying the book of Daniel."

Daniel smiled and nodded politely. He didn't mind a bit of human interaction, but he wasn't about to let the whole town know his business, which was sure to happen if he started gabbing it up with the locals.

Gabbing it up? Where did that come from? He wondered. Oh, yes, Ms. Pat, his waitress last night at the diner. When his food practically got cold as she was trying to wangle information out of him, she finally apologized for gabbing it up and keeping him from his dinner.

Reverend Sam chuckled. "I see you went to the Main Street Diner. Ms. Pat is always gabbing it up, isn't she? Ha-ha!"

Emma hadn't had time to do much besides get supplies and get the inn ready, so she hadn't been to the diner. "Are you kidding? Ms. Pat is still waiting tables there? I thought she'd be retired by now."

"No, my dear, she's still running the good race," the reverend smiled. "She likes it there, says it keeps her mind from going stale, remembering orders and gabbing it up with the customers. Besides, she's only my age, you know."

That put Emma on the spot all right. She fought the urge to say, "Okay, boomer," and just smiled. "I'll have to drop by and say hello. She was always very kind to me and Olivia after Mom died."

"Yes, she's a good egg," replied Reverend Sam. "So," he addressed Daniel and Emma. "Let's all take a seat and say grace so we can get started on those muffins."

—⁂—

"I'm afraid the renovations might disturb you. I know you came here for peace and quiet," Emma said after they had finished their light breakfast and were washing up in the kitchen. It was unusual for a guest to help out, but Daniel had insisted, something about making up for scaring the wits out of her earlier.

"Well, that depends on how involved the renovations get. If we're talking hammering and sawing then yes, I'd probably have to find somewhere else to stay. If it's just painting and wallpapering though, I'm sure I'll be fine."

As an architect, Emma was afraid there would indeed be hammering and sawing, but she didn't want him to leave just yet. She liked this man, felt at ease around him. She wasn't after a lifelong romance – not after her last relationship went sour. What she craved was friendship. Sure, he was just a guest, so there were boundaries, but she enjoyed his company without thinking too far ahead. Indeed, she thought of the Scripture Ecclesiastes 3:1: "To everything there is a season, and a time for every purpose under heaven." But all she said was,

"I'm not sure how much space you need. We do have the garden shed and a small greenhouse. When the weather is good, you could maybe paint or sketch out there. My family isn't into hoarding or stockpiling or anything like that. As you can see, we just have a few nice pieces around that my grandparents collected plus the essentials in here. It's the same in the shed. Plenty of workspace."

Daniel tilted his head and seemed to gaze into the distance as he pondered. *That's kind of cute,* Emma thought, *but could get annoying if he zones out all the time.*

"We'll see," was all he said. She wondered what that meant but the dishes were done and put away and there was no further reason to hang around the kitchen together. Plus, she had things she needed to do regarding the renovations.

"Okay, well, thanks for helping with the cleanup. You know you don't have to do that every day. You're a guest here. We don't want it spread on social media that we make our guests work for their room and board," she joked. "I'm going to start a task list for the renovations and find some local workers to take care of things. We'll be as quiet as we can."

"I appreciate that. If it gets to be too much, I'll let you know. Until then, I'll just take a walk and maybe check out that shed if you don't mind."

"Please, go right ahead. If you think it will work for you, we can do some light renovations in there as well to make it more comfortable for you."

She realized it was a bit much to offer so much to a guest at the inn she hardly knew. She rationalized it aloud. "You know, because it's a pretty old building, built by my grandfather. And some other guests might want to use it to. My sister, Olivia, could use it for writing her magazine articles –" Emma stopped herself. She was starting to blither, as her dad called it. Something about some guy named the Fonz...

"Okay, thanks again, and I'll see you at breakfast. I'll be much more prepared tomorrow."

He chuckled. *Did he just blush?*

The next morning, breakfast did go a lot more smoothly. Emma made a French toast casserole and made sure to straighten up the kitchen before Daniel came down. Part of her liked the fact that he helped out with cleaning up, but another part really was worried it might end up on social media. #MustWorkForFood. After all, they really didn't know much about the man.

Olivia would be arriving today. Emma was relieved, as she was finding it a stretch to both plan the renovations and take care of the cooking and housekeeping, even if it was just for the one guest.

"That was delicious, Emma, thank you. So, what's the plan for today?" asked Reverend Sam as he wiped his mouth with his napkin.

"Yes, Emma, thank you," agreed Daniel. "If you don't need me for cleanup duty, I've got some phone calls to make."

"Nope, it was just one pan and it's soaking now, so you're off the hook," Emma smiled. Daniel rose and nodded to Emma and Reverend Samuel and made his way upstairs.

She turned to her dad. "Today I'll interview some of the local handymen who might want to give a quote for the renovation work. Maybe hire one or two of them, depending on their skills. I found some soft areas in some of the corners of the upstairs rooms that will need carpentry work, and the guest bedrooms need new paint and window coverings, as well as bed covers and pictures. I'll leave Grandma's vases and figurines out though, they add a special touch, I think."

"That's nice, but it sounds expensive. How are we planning to pay for all this?" replied the reverend pensively.

"Well, I can't speak for Olivia, but the rent I would have been paying in the city can be used better here. I gave up my apartment, Dad. I'm planning to stay for the long haul."

Tears brimmed in Reverend Sam's eyes and threatened to spill over. He cleared his throat. "You're a good daughter, Emma. You are a heritage from the Lord," he said, quoting from Psalm 127:3. He gave Emma a quick squeeze on the shoulder. "Now let's get about our duties for the day."

—⁂—

"Hey, anybody home?" came a cheerful voice from the front hallway.

"Olivia!" Emma cheered. Her sister was home. Emma rushed to greet her and they hugged as if they hadn't just talked that morning. FaceTime and texting only go so far, but when someone you love is finally right there in front of you, well, hugging is required.

"How was the drive?" she asked. "Are you hungry? Tired? Do you need a rest? Did you stop by the church to see Dad?"

"Whoa there, Nellie. Yes, I'm hungry. Yes, I'm tired. No, I don't need a rest. No, I did not stop by the church," Olivia replied as she set down her backpack. They both looked at each other and laughed.

"I'm sorry, I'm just so glad you're here. I feel like God brought us home to circle the wagons or something. I can't explain it."

"Why, is something wrong with Dad?" Olivia asked, levity gone and concern etched in her face.

"No, nothing like that. It just seems odd that at this stage of our lives we're both able to make it work, I mean, coming home like this to be together as a family. I'm sure I'm reading more into it than I need to."

"Yes, you're probably stressed from having so much on your plate. Plus the big move from the city back home. Plus, you know...Byron."

Emma sighed. "Well, now that you're here, we can share the load. You'd better brace yourself before we go into the office though. The books" – she made air quotes around books – "were mostly just sticky notes. Nothing seems amiss, but I'll need help organizing them. Also help with the website, and by help, I mean you." She smiled and gave Olivia a hopeful look.

"You got it, sis. I feel the same way, like we're here for a reason. I thought it was just to save the inn but maybe there is a life lesson God wants us to learn here." For someone as pragmatic as a journalist, Olivia had a very strong faith that Emma admired.

From upstairs, the girls heard a loud male voice. The floor creaked above them, back and forth. Daniel was obviously pacing.

"Look, Izzy, I told you, I need a break." A long silence. "What you did was wrong –" A shorter silence. "No, don't –" An exasperated sigh and no more pacing.

Emma and Olivia didn't mean to eavesdrop, but it couldn't be helped. They looked up and then at each other and decided to quietly head to the kitchen.

"That's Daniel Reynolds, in the guest room at the top of the stairs," Emma said in response to Olivia's raised eyebrows. "He must have been making a cell phone call. The signal's not so good here. That must be why he was talking so loud."

"True," Olivia agreed, grabbing an apple from the bowl on the counter. "Let's go take a walk. We don't want him to think we overheard him on purpose."

The girls headed out the back door. It was partly sunny and no breeze, but still a bit chilly. "Let's go check out the garden shed and greenhouse," Emma suggested. "I told Daniel he could use it as an art studio if the renovations get too loud. It may need a coat of paint or some fixing up to make it useable."

They made their way through the garden to the shed and opened the door. It creaked and threatened to fall off its hinges. "Well, new hinges will be needed, and the door jamb might need to be replaced as well, it looks a bit soggy," noted Emma.

"It is pretty bright in here though, and look, the greenhouse could be used as a solarium as well as starting seedlings," Olivia added, looking through the back door to the attached greenhouse.

Emma looked around the interior of the shed. "Looks like some rot in the walls where the heater vents out," she said, pressing lightly on the wall.

"Hello?" Daniel's voice called from outside the shed.

"Hi, Daniel, come on in," Emma replied.

Daniel stepped through the door and looked around. Olivia smiled and held out her hand. "Hi, I'm Olivia. You must be Daniel."

"Yes, hi, Olivia, nice to meet you," Daniel said, shaking her hand. He noticed her mannerism was so much like Reverend Sam's. "I needed some air and heard voices, so thought I'd check it out."

Emma and Olivia tried hard not to make eye contact and confirm their guilt at overhearing his conversation, which only made it clear to Daniel that they had indeed heard.

"I was on the phone with my art dealer. She wants me to produce more for her to sell but I told her I just need a break right now. She's very... persuasive," he added, running his hand through his hair.

Now Emma and Olivia couldn't help but look at each other, each trying to keep a straight face.

"Well," Emma responded, "I think this shed will work fine for you to take your break. And when the inspiration hits, you can draw or paint as you like.

Daniel took a look around, noting the windows and natural lighting. He liked what he saw, except the rot under the windowsill.

Emma saw his eyes stop there and she bent down to take a closer look. "Uh-oh, looks like there's a bit more than paint needed here." She pressed on it and her hand went straight through the drywall.

"Oh! I didn't realize it was that bad." Emma retracted her hand.

"Are you all right?" asked Olivia, rushing over to help her sister.

"Yes, I'm fine. This will all have to be replaced." Emma started pulling at the drywall. Daniel crouched down to help, widening the hole.

"Hey, what's this?" Olivia reached her hand into the hole and pulled out a tin that probably once held chocolate or cookies. She tried to open it. "The lid is rusted shut."

"Here, let me try," Daniel offered. He managed to loosen one corner of the tin at a time until finally, it popped off. The three of them looked inside, then looked up at each other, astounded.

Inside the tin was a yellowed envelope with faded cursive writing on the front. "*To My One True Love...*"

CHAPTER 4

FAMILY TIES

All heads turned as the Dodge Charger came roaring through the center of town, not even pretending to slow down at the crosswalks. The chugging of the engine reverberated off the brick and cement facades of the old buildings facing Main Street.

In the diner, patrons stopped with forks in midair, mouths agape. This was not an everyday occurrence in the small town of Graceville.

Daniel was in the middle of the diner's lunch special when the Charger barreled past the window where he was seated. A slight feeling of despair overcame him. He knew the driver all too well. *Izzy.* She'd found him.

He knew where she was headed and sure enough, the sound of the Charger down-shifting, idling, and ending, indicated she had, in fact, gone directly to the Turner Inn.

Once the commotion died down, the conversations in the diner resumed only this time, all the talk was about the new stranger in town.

"Did you see that? I hope there's not a hot rod car show coming through town."

"Do you think it's a drug dealer?"

Old Gus, there on his lunch break, just smiled and thought to himself, *Ah, I used to have an original one of those. Yep, 1966 was a very good year for cars.*

Ms. Pat came over to refresh Daniel's coffee. She did not wait tables anymore, but helped out as hostess and cashier, filling coffee cups – and sometimes giving sage advice – as needed.

"Well now, I've seen everything," Ms. Pat began as she poured steaming-hot coffee into Daniel's cup without even asking. "That maniac must think they're still in the city, driving like that. Some of these old brick streets are a hundred years old, they cain't stand that kind of abuse."

Daniel, usually quite reticent, absentmindedly said, "Yes, she's abusive all right."

"She?" Ms. Pat was quick to pick up. "You know her?"

Daniel blushed, immediately realizing his mistake. Luckily, Ms. Pat was not a gossip. Well, she didn't gossip *too* much. "Yes, she is – was – my art dealer."

Ms. Pat nodded knowingly but the blank look in her eyes gave her away.

"She arranges events where I can display my artwork and finds buyers so I can concentrate on the art itself instead of the marketing and sales."

The light went on in Ms. Pat's eyes. "Oh, yes, I see. I knew you were an artist, but I didn't know you were a *big* artist." She looked out the window down the street toward the inn. "What's she doing here? I thought you were on vacation."

"Yes, well..." Daniel began to squirm. He'd already released too much information and didn't know how to get out of this trap he'd made for himself without being rude. "We, that is, she and I... we..."

Ms. Pat caught on and put Daniel out of his misery. "Oh, now I really *do* see. You and she are an item."

"*Were* an item," Daniel quickly interjected. "Relationships are tough enough already, but when you add business into the personal nature of a man and woman trying to be a couple, it can get...complicated."

Ms. Pat nodded as they both gazed out the window in the direction of the Turner Inn.

Unbeknownst to either of them, Avery Thompson, sitting at the next table over, heard every word.

—⁂—

Emma sat on the front porch in one of the rocking chairs. She had finished her morning chores, ate a small lunch, and wanted to rest but then thought better of it, knowing her habit of procrastination. She thought to herself, she might have to start looking for help quickly or she would definitely push herself to exhaustion. She had accepted these facts about herself and when she recognized shortcomings, she strove to overcome them.

There was something about the motion of rocking that relaxes the muscles and the mind. She began to reminisce about her childhood in Graceville, and how so many things had changed…and how so many had not.

Grandma and Grandpa always took time in the evening to sit in these rockers and talk about the day behind them and what lay ahead. Emma and Olivia would usually play on the steps. Not dolls, but other games of imagination like trying to count the number of leaves on the trees or, if it was Christmas, trying to count the number of Christmas trees you passed as you rode somewhere, or ask weird questions about the universe. Dad would usually be running a Bible study class or doing other "church work," as he called it. Of course, Mom was gone by then, having passed from cancer when Olivia was only five years old.

Emma had given up on asking, "Where's Mommy?" long before. In truth, she resented the church a bit for taking him away from her. She felt like she had lost both parents when Mom died. Reverend Sam buried himself in his work after her death, staying away all day and half the night.

Emma remained unaware that his avoidance stemmed from an inability to confront the emptiness of Barbara's chair each day, and clung to the solace of merely clutching her pillow every night.

Grandma passed away too, leaving Emma and Olivia with no mother figure. Grandpa would often tell stories about Grandma and their ancestors who had come to Graceville when it was "little more than a stop on the Pony Express" Grandpa would say.

Their people had come over from Great Britain in the early 1800s, some of the first settlers to arrive in the area. The town was, indeed, a stop on the Pony Express, but that wasn't enough to make it a boom town.

The area was beautiful, bountiful, and indeed, was the main attraction. It was near enough to the big cities on either side of it to get supplies in and send their children to college, but small enough to be more of a resort town that managed to keep its quaintness – by virtue of lack of technological infrastructure upgrades, as evidenced by the internet connection problems most people had.

Emma's great-great-grandparents had opened the inn before the term *bed and breakfast* was even invented. That was when the house, garden, and shed were built. The walking paths were put in as time and money allowed. They made it through the Great Depression, and the Turner Inn still boasted quite a bit of the Depression glassware and other useful items from that time. They even still used some of their vintage motorized bicycles, the predecessors to mopeds, to get around town.

What *had* changed for the better was Emma and her dad's relationship. During her rebellious teenage years, she had confronted him, accusing him of not caring about her or Olivia. She cringed inwardly remembering that afternoon...

Emma looked up from the book she was reading at the kitchen table as Reverend Samuel walked in. "What are you doing here?"

"Um, I live here," her dad replied. He could sense the tension in his daughter and wished more than ever that his wife was here to help their daughters through puberty.

"Surprised to see you, that's all." Emma returned to her book.

"I'm just here for lunch, then I have to get back."

"Oh, sure, your 'church work.'" She made air quotes with her free hand.

"Honey—"

That was all it took.

"No, Dad, don't bother. I've heard it all before. Your parishioners need you, I get it. But did you ever stop to think that I need you too? That Olivia needs you? You disappeared after Mom died. You're never home. It's like you never even loved her, you just went back to work!"

And that was all it took for the reverend.

"Never loved her? Never loved her!" he sputtered. "Young lady, I don't ever want to hear you say that again. I loved your mother more than anything except God. I lost almost everything when I lost her. You have no idea, and no right to accuse me of such a thing!"

He composed himself a bit.

"You're very young, I get it, and you miss her too. You read a lot, but you know nothing about..."

He stopped himself. If she knew nothing about love, it was his fault. He was her father. Yes, Barbara should have been the one to have "the talk" with their daughters, but it would apparently be up to him.

Emma just looked at him with a mixture of scorn, fear, and longing in her eyes. True, she did read a lot and thought she knew everything – well, a lot, anyway.

She feared her father not in a physical way, but more of a respectful way, like she feared God, but on a smaller scale.

And she longed for him to just hold her like when she was a little girl and tell her everything would be all right, Mom would be coming home soon and everything would be the way it used to be. But she knew that would never happen.

The lump in her throat kept her from speaking but the quiver in her lip and the tears welling in her eyes said it all. Reverend Sam did scoop her up and held her close, rocking her back and forth a bit as they both released the tears they were holding back.

"Honey, I'm sorry. My heart was so broken, I just went on autopilot, leaving your grandparents to take care of you.

"Look, how about if we both try again. You're growing up so fast, I don't really know what to do."

Emma was a bit shaken by that remark. Her dad, the reverend and leader of a congregation, didn't know what to do? But at the same time, he acknowledged she was growing up, so she felt she could handle it.

Reverend Sam backed up a bit and held her by the shoulders at arm's length. "Let's have a talk. Your mom should be doing this, but I'll give it a try."

Emma nodded and they both stepped out onto the back porch and started off down one of the garden paths.

—⁓—

The aroma of coffee once again lured Daniel out of his room and toward the dining room. He'd managed to avoid Izzy last night by staying at the library until they closed, then sneaking in as best he could what with the squeaky floors and creaking hinges.

The librarian, Miss Evelyn Miller, was delightful. Her bright-blue eyes glistened behind her rimless spectacles and the hand-made lace collar of her dress reminded Daniel of days gone by. She'd greeted him quietly but warmly and directed him to the reading room.

Daniel braced himself for what was surely to be a showdown at breakfast. Izzy would be there, and she would not be happy finding out that he had tried hard to avoid her and had actually gone to a lot of trouble to do so.

In the dining room sat Reverend Samuel, Emma, and Izzy. It was apparently Olivia's turn to make breakfast. An array of cereal, juice, and milk sat on the sideboard along with coffee, hot water, and an assortment of teas. Some yogurt and fresh fruit in small bowls were available as a healthy option to start the day.

"Ah, speak of the devil," Reverend Turner greeted Daniel. "Just a figure of speech," he explained as Daniel's eyes grew a bit wide. He grinned.

"Good morning, Daniel," Emma cut in. Sometimes her father's humor was beyond her. "Meet Isabella Thornton. She'll be staying with us for about a week. Miss Thornton, meet Daniel Reynolds."

Before Daniel could say anything, Izzy exclaimed, "It's so nice to meet you, Mr. Reynolds. Please, call me Izzy."

Daniel was perplexed. What was up with this act? Why didn't she just admit they knew each other? Should he go along with it? He didn't think it was wise to lie to these fine people.

"Izzy—" he began, but she cut him off.

"Since you've been here a week or so already, maybe you could show me around the grounds." She stood up and before he knew it was standing next to him with her arm in his, guiding him toward the door.

The coffee would have to wait.

—◊—

"What was that all about?" he questioned as soon as they were out of earshot. "Why are you pretending we don't know each other?"

"Well," Izzy purred, clenching her fingers into his arm a bit too tightly, "those nice church people spoke very highly of you. A polite young man, an artist, here for a respite from city life. If they learned of our affair, how long do you think they'd let you stay here? I just thought I'd keep that information to myself until the time is right."

"Until the time is right? Are you blackmailing me? What is it you want? What are you here for? Never mind that, how did you find me?"

"My, my, so many questions. Let's see, last question first. I found you through your neighbor, the one you use to watch your cat when you're away. It was a piece of cake.

"What is it I want and what am I here for? I want you back, and I'm here for you. I'm not accustomed to being dumped and losing a prime client all in one go. I'm happy to let you stay here and get your head clear and come to your senses, but then I want you back in the city, with me as your lover *and* your agent.

"As for blackmail, that's such an ugly word." She snickered. "Let's just say I want what I want, and I know how to get it."

CHAPTER 5

SECRETS IN THE LETTERS

E mma stood in the kitchen, bleary-eyed. Her father's cheery, "Time to make the donuts!" had long since lost its hilarity.

Thankfully, today's breakfast would be fairly simple. The menu consisted of breakfast sandwiches on English muffins, coffee, juice, scrambled eggs, and store-bought hash browns. For a sweet ending, she'd also put out yogurt with fresh fruit.

Olivia was vegan, so she'd brought some fake sausage patties she'd found (no pun intended) that tasted just like the real thing but without any gristle. It was a new brand, Nature's Fynd, so could still be purchased at the low introductory price. The other guests would have that plus real eggs and cheddar cheese, while Olivia would have Just Egg and plant-based cheese.

Emma debated whether to tell her guests the truth about the sausage, then decided to casually mention it after the meal. She was just too tired to make two different sausages, plus the clean-up afterward. Her conscience still niggled at her. Was that a sin of omission? Is delay a sin? She'd think about that later. Right now, it was time to make the donuts...er, brew the coffee.

She'd been going over the food budget and thanks to Daniel's and now Izzy's unexpected bookings, the inn would be able to afford a part-time cook soon. She and Olivia would still need to share the housekeeping duties for the time being, but that was doable and helped them to keep on top of tasks throughout the inn that had previously been overlooked. As they say, two sets of eyes are better than one and it also gave them the perspective that their clients would have while staying. This also guaranteed top-notch service, as they would not be dependent on others to ensure everything was in perfect condition for their revamped approach.

At 6:45 a.m. she started hearing the floors creaking upstairs. Her guests were getting ready to come down for breakfast. She pressed start on the toaster oven for the English muffins, heated the oil in the pan for the fake sausage, used the pancake skillet and egg rings for the eggs, and had the cheese slices ready for assembly. Actually, everything would be ready at the same time, four minutes for everything. Emma thought...*If everyone enjoys this meal, it will become a staple for mornings that I am running short on time or even want to sleep in a bit.*

—⁕—

Daniel listened at his door in case he heard Izzy in the hallway. He really wanted to avoid her but he was the one who chose this delightful inn for a getaway, so why should he forego breakfast? *She* should be the one eating at the diner. Besides, she'd just follow him there if he left the inn now.

It seemed quiet out in the hallway, so he tried to open his door without squeaking or clicking the mechanism but no chance, with a rattle and a creak, the door opened. The coast looked clear, so Daniel stepped out into the hallway, closing the door behind him and heading for the stairs.

He'd just begun to relax, thinking maybe Izzy had given up when there she was, suddenly appearing at the bottom of the staircase. What was she doing, hiding? There was no escape.

He squared his shoulders and raised his head high. He'd made the decision to tell the family of his and Izzy's past and let the chips fall where they may. They might ask him to leave, which would be their right. After all, this was a pastor's house and he and this woman had just engaged in a conversation with them where each stated they did not know the other. They may feel that there could be underlying drama and not trust them to be there at the inn.

Worse than being asked to leave would be to fall from their good graces. They had welcomed him into their home and made him feel comfortable. They didn't know he'd just been through torment with Izzy and was essentially running away from his problems. They and the inn were just what he needed at a very low point in his life.

He'd just begun to process his feelings about Izzy and their breakup when she showed up and put him in a tailspin. But it confirmed what he already knew: Izzy was not the woman he wanted to spend the rest of his life with. In fact, he didn't even really want to share a meal with her but...the coffee aroma wafting from downstairs was so alluring. *Is coffee addiction a sin?* He'd have to consult the reverend on that issue.

Izzy held out her hand to Daniel as he reached the bottom of the stairs. He just stared at her in disbelief. She was not accepting the fact that they were over. And he wouldn't be blackmailed by her, no matter what she chose to call it.

Izzy put her hand down and shrugged, a smirk on her face as if to say, fine, but I'll get you yet. She tried walking beside him through the doorway but the pocket doors weren't fully open and they both couldn't fit. They didn't exactly get stuck, but it was more than awkward as they tried to extract themselves. Izzy's composure slipped a bit as she slightly ricocheted and her shoulder hit the partially open door. She bounced back into Daniel and tilted a little bit backwards. After she regained her footing and gave a silent glare, Daniel gallantly stepped back and held out a hand with a flourish, gesturing Izzy through the doorway.

Reverend Sam was already seated at the dining room table and tried very hard not to laugh. This was the second time Daniel had entered the dining room and flummoxed a lady upon his arrival. The last time it was Emma, and she almost dropped the tray of coffee and tea.

In that instance though, Daniel had been mortified by the accident he almost caused and apologized profusely. This time, the reverend could sense real animosity, although he tried to hide it. *There's more to this story than meets the eye.*

"Good morning, Daniel, Miss Izzy," greeted the reverend. "I trust you slept well?"

Izzy plastered a smile on her makeup-covered face. "Oh, yes, this country air really is so good for my complexion and it is so quiet here. I slept like a *baby*." She glanced at Daniel slyly. He used to call her baby, and she added that in just to annoy him.

Before Daniel could respond, Olivia came bouncing in. "Good

morning, everyone! Isn't it a beautiful day?" She walked over and gave her dad a kiss on the cheek. "I'll go see if Emma needs a hand." She went through the swinging door into the kitchen.

Daniel decided to wait until the whole family was present to come clean and let them know collectively that he and Izzy knew each other. He went to the sideboard to pour his coffee. His hands were shaking. This meant more to him than he even realized. Was it because of not wanting to let the reverend down? Or was it because of Emma?

Where did that come from? Yes, Emma was delightful, and pretty, and smart. But he knew better than to jump into a new relationship after the last one ended so badly. Besides, she had the power over his housing at the moment, and he wasn't going to mess with that.

Izzy sidled up to him, a little too close, and reached across him to get a cup and saucer, brushing his torso with her arm. She tried to make eye contact but Daniel just shook his head and sat down at the table.

"Good morning, Reverend," Daniel said after finally getting a breath. "Yes, I slept well, thank you."

"So, what do you young people have planned for today?"

Daniel quickly turned his head. "What do you mean?"

Reverend Sam looked puzzled. "Nothing, just making conversation. Miss Izzy might be going sightseeing and needing some directions, and you might be painting or sketching. Although, it might get a bit noisy when the renovations start, and I don't want you to be disturbed. That's all."

Daniel was embarrassed. He was too on edge. He had to get this knowing Izzy thing off his conscience. Maybe he should do a private confession with the reverend in his office? He thought about the verse in 1 John 1:9. "If we confess our sins, He is faithful and righteous to forgive us our sins and to cleanse us from all unrighteousness." No, he wanted Emma to know and for that matter, Olivia might as well know too. They needed to hear it from him before Izzy made up some story that was even worse than the truth, although that would be difficult.

Just at that moment, Emma and Olivia entered the dining room with trays of what looked like McMuffins and some yogurt and fruit. "Breakfast is served!" announced Olivia, too cheerful in contrast to Emma's fatigue.

"Good morning, Daniel, Izzy. Please help yourselves to a sandwich and some yogurt."

Izzy didn't wait and just reached across the table and grabbed a sandwich. She immediately stuck it in her mouth and took a huge bite. "Mmm," was all she could manage with her mouth so full.

The others were a bit surprised and embarrassed for her as Emma and Olivia took their seats and bowed their heads, waiting for the reverend to say grace. Daniel tried not to laugh but was secretly pleased she had made a fool of herself, then quickly became contrite knowing it was not nice to revel in others' misfortunes. He remembered Proverbs 24:17: "Don't rejoice when your enemies fall; don't be happy when they stumble." He bowed his head.

Olivia, realizing her mistake, bowed her head also and tried to chew as unobtrusively as possible. The reverend said a very short grace, trying to ease her discomfort. After all, she was a guest in their home, a paying customer of the inn, and it was his job to bring comfort. Usually. The reverend was aware that discomfort produced growth in most cases, but this young lady was a guest, and he did not know her well at all.

—⁂—

Daniel couldn't bring himself to tell the family at breakfast about his and Izzy's connection. Izzy was quiet after her faux pas and Olivia was engaged in pleasant chatter, and he did not want to disrupt the moment. He resolved to tell them tomorrow.

Meanwhile, the reverend went to the rectory to do his church business. Izzy escaped to her room. Olivia and Emma were interviewing local contractors for the renovations. Emma had developed a To-Do list of items she thought they could take care of in phase one, then after getting more paying guests, they could proceed to other phases. The most expensive items, a new roof and windows, would come last.

Daniel planned to go to the garden shed to set up his easels. He wanted to be ready to start drawing when the inspiration struck him. He'd decided to go with charcoal for this stage of his career: black and chalky.

Someday, he envisioned himself returning to the use of deep, rich oils; however, for the present, the stark contrast of black on white resonated with his pursuit of unraveling life's simple truths, particularly those pertinent to his current existence. Maybe in his declining years he'd go for pastel watercolors, who knew?

After he got settled in the shed, he gazed out the window. It certainly was a beautiful day, with the sun shining and the birds chirping. It would be spring soon. Maybe he'd move on from his charcoal phase sooner than he thought.

He was startled out of his reverie by the sound of boots clomping outside and voices coming closer. The door opened and in walked Emma and Olivia, followed by a contractor.

"Oh!" said Emma, blushing. "I'm so sorry, Daniel, I didn't know you were in here. We'll come back later—"

"No need, I haven't started anything yet, just getting set up."

The contractor was taking in everything; the handsome young man who was a guest at the inn, his art setup…the way Miss Emma blushed when she spoke to him. Hmm, he'd have to run this by his wife to see what she thought.

Daniel looked at his watch. "The library will be open in about an hour. Maybe I can just use one of the mopeds and drive around town until Ms. Miller arrives to open the doors." He'd come to know the librarian, Evelyn Miller, through using the library's reading room.

The last time they were in the garden shed, they'd found the letter addressed: *To My One True Love.* They'd opened the yellowed envelope only to find a vague few lines with no name at the top or signature at the bottom.

I love you more than you could know. You came with me here to this place to escape the ungodly. I know I shall prosper with your blessing.

Was this some kind of Underground Railway station stop at one time? Or a former prostitute trying to change her ways? They might never find the answer. For now, it was a mystery.

"Yes, of course, I'm sorry we bothered you." She began to usher the contractor out. "We're just about finished here anyway." She pointed out the rot under the window and noted, "That's the kind of thing we need to have fixed at this stage."

The contractor nodded and was ushered outside. "No problem, Miss Emma, I'll write up a quote and get it to you in the morning." He tipped his hat and walked over to his pickup truck. He hoped to get this job; there were a lot of small projects he could easily take care of, and maybe find out a little more about this stranger and the goings-on at the inn.

CHAPTER 6

BUSINESS RIVALRY

With the contractors gone and the inn's chores mostly done, Emma decided to take a walk around the grounds. With a warm cup of herbal tea in hand, she started making her way down one of the pea stone paths her grandparents had created back during the Great Depression.

It must have been awfully difficult during that time; different than post-pandemic, but just as scary. She wondered how her grandparents had kept the inn afloat back then. Maybe if she could find out, it would help them get back to the black, because many of the budget reports she printed out showed they were in the red.

That was actually a great idea, finding out how they'd managed back in the 1930s. Some of the concepts and procedures could surely be updated to help the Turner Inn today. She'd speak to Olivia about it. Being a journalist, Olivia would know better how to delve through records to find things out.

As Emma turned a bend in the path, stones crunching under her feet, she took in a view of the inn from that angle. It warmed her heart and at the same time created anxiety. Warmth from memories of her mostly happy childhood – barring her mother's untimely death – and anxiety that she didn't want the family inn to have to close on her watch.

When her father sent out his distress call to her, it couldn't have come at a better time. She needed to get out of the city, away from Byron, her ex-boyfriend, and all the hustle and bustle and just give her heart and mind time to heal. Besides, so many people were working from home now and conducting business online, it hardly mattered.

Emma suspected Reverend Turner also wanted his daughter home for safekeeping. He had to have suspected trouble in paradise from her lack of emails and phone calls as she dealt with her romantic troubles.

Back to the view of the inn, she could see some of the dormers and turrets and the widow's walk over the tree line. The weathervane had long since blown down; maybe that was something they could address during the roof renovations a few years from now.

Thankfully, the paint didn't look too bad. It was still white with black trim, no peeling, just a little bit of oxidation. The red front door gave it a classic look.

Uh-oh... there looked to be some rot under one of the attic windows. She must have missed that on a previous walkabout, or maybe it was new. She mentally added that to her to-do list.

Rounding another bend heading back toward the house, she happened to pass by the garden shed just as Daniel was exiting. "Oh, hello!" she said. "I hope I didn't disturb you."

"Not at all, I was just taking a break. It looks like another gorgeous day with spring on the way. Is the weather always like this here?" he asked.

"Not always, although we are sheltered quite a bit in this valley. I think we'll have an early spring. Olivia will say it's climate change, but I'm looking forward to the lilacs blooming."

Daniel nodded as they began to stroll toward the house. "How are the renovations coming?" He half-hoped she'd say they'd have to ask Izzy to leave the inn to make way for construction, but also knew that was the coward's way out. He couldn't run from his problems; in fact, they'd followed him here. *She'd* followed him here. He still hadn't had a chance to tell the family that he and Izzy were previously an item, and the guilt was starting to pile up on him, weighing heavily on his conscience like a millstone in the sea (Matt. 18:6).

Before she could answer, he decided to come clean. "The reason I ask is that, I think you should know that, well..."

His usually calm demeanor had changed and Emma noticed it. He was suddenly very uncomfortable. She paused and turned toward him, wondering what he was going to say.

He cleared his throat. "You see, well..."

She arched her eyebrows as an indication he should continue.

"Well, you see..." This was getting him nowhere.

"Well, back in the city, well..."

Emma was a patient woman but was starting to lose it. "Daniel, just spit it out."

"Okay. Back in the city, I wasn't exactly a poor, starving artist…"

"I gathered as much from your expensive luggage and watch. There's no need to explain. Your money is your business —"

"Yes, that's exactly it. My business is making art, and my business manager is — was — Izzy."

Now Emma was confused. "So, you know each other? Why did you pretend you didn't?"

"I don't know. When she acted like we didn't know each other, I wasn't sure what she was planning, so I just sort of went along with it. The truth is, we were more than just business partners."

The light began to dawn on Emma. "Oh, I see, so, you were a couple?"

This wasn't going as badly as Daniel thought. "Yes, we were a couple. But it ended pretty badly. She's more interested in my art than in me. And…" *Out with it!* "And I didn't want to disappoint your dad by letting on that we, well, we actually lived together for a while." He looked relieved but expectant as he finished his confession, wondering what her reaction would be. Would she throw him out? Or tell her father and *he'd* throw him out? Whatever the consequences, at least he'd come clean, and he felt good about that.

Emma had a number of emotions going through her, but her face remained outwardly calm while her heartbeat quickened. Admiration was her first response. This near-stranger had a past with a woman and respected her father the reverend so much, he was ashamed to admit it. Someone like that was hard to find in these "fast and loose" times, as her dad would say.

Surprisingly, or maybe not, her second emotion was jealousy. That should have surprised her but didn't. She'd been ignoring her growing feelings for Daniel. He was a guest at the inn, number one. And a stranger, number two. And she was trying to heal from her own romantic misadventure, number three. And she needed to concentrate on getting the inn back on her feet, for her family's sake.

Then came the anger that he had lied to her, or at least omitted the truth. Was it such a big deal though? She was torn. He had every right to reveal or hide whatever he wished. Logically, it didn't matter what his past was as long as he paid his bed and breakfast bill. But deep down, she yearned for him to embody the role of a gallant knight in shining armor, only to confront the harsh reality that he was merely a mortal man, subject to flaws and limitations like any other.

As she grappled with the overwhelming sense that the Holy Spirit was guiding her, she gently addressed Daniel, 'Daniel, remember the words of Psalm 103:12, "As far as the east is from the west, so far has he removed our transgressions from us." You owe us no explanations for your past; forgiveness and understanding are freely given. However, honesty is paramount, and I urge you to disclose this to Dad. Let the truth set you free from the burden of deception." The last word she spoke carried a sharp edge, a realization that didn't escape her. Despite her awareness, it emerged instinctively, propelled by emotions she struggled to contain.

Daniel flinched slightly at the words, but he squared his jaw and nodded in agreement.

Although the reverend's judgment was paramount, revealing the truth to Emma sparked a revelation within him: her opinion held profound importance. It extended beyond the fear of her dismissal and possible eviction from the inn; rather, he craved her respect and admiration, understanding that their relationship held deeper significance than he had previously acknowledged.

"I'll go over to the church right now. I originally intended to broach this topic over breakfast tomorrow, but now that I've initiated the process, delaying the completion serves no purpose—it's time to rip off the Band-Aid completely."

"Good idea. I'm sure Dot, his receptionist, can find some time on his calendar for you. See you later." Emma headed toward the house with her now-cold cup of tea in hand while Daniel headed off in the direction of the church.

—∞—

Dot did indeed usher Daniel in to see Reverend Turner just a few moments after he arrived. Daniel had stood awkwardly at first, now facing the man whose opinion mattered to him more than he thought it should. Daniel's upbringing may have contributed to his current demeanor, particularly considering the absence of his own father during his younger years.

The reverend sensed his discomfort and took a more ministerial approach rather than just the head of the table at breakfast. "Sit down, son. What's on your mind?"

"Well, sir, it's like this. Izzy –" He stopped himself. He wasn't going to place all the blame on Izzy to try to keep his own reputation intact. He'd gone along with her ruse and would take the blame for his part in it.

"That is, I actually know Izzy. We pretended we didn't know each other... I'm not sure why." That wasn't true. He couldn't compound an omission with an outright lie. Suddenly, the words started flowing from his mouth. "That's not true. I do know why, but I'm not at liberty to say. What I can tell you is that Izzy was my business manager in the city." The reverend looked at him questioningly. "She sold my artwork for me." The reverend nodded. "We were also a couple." The reverend waited patiently for what he suspected was coming. "And for a while, we lived together." Daniel stopped talking.

The reverend steepled his fingers together in thought. It was usually a good idea to not rush these things.

"I see. And you're telling me this because...?"

"Because I respect you as a reverend, and as an innkeeper. I'm under your roof, and I thought you should know the truth."

"Have you told Emma?" The reverend hadn't noticed anything untoward in Emma and Daniel's behavior, but he had noticed the occasional glance at each other when each thought the other wasn't looking. He hadn't said anything, but in his heart, he thought these two young people might be a good match.

Daniel was surprised by the question, only coming to realize a few moments before that his feelings for Emma were... well, feelings.

"Yes, it was her idea that I come here to tell you right away rather than waiting."

"Good, good," said the reverend, leaning back in his chair. "So you thought I'd find out about your past and judge you? Maybe ask you to leave the inn?"

Wow, he's good. "Yes, sir. But mostly, I didn't want your opinion of me to lessen. Or Emma's. If you do want me to leave, just let me know and I'll settle my bill —"

"No need for that, my boy. I'm glad you said something. God doesn't like deception, and neither do I. But it seems like the Holy Spirit convicted you to let me know, and I can tell it wasn't easy. I respect you for that. You did the right thing.

"I'm not here to judge anyone, I'm here to help lead people to God through Jesus. We're all sinners; that's why Jesus died for us on the cross, to redeem our sins and bring us closer to our heavenly Father.

"The Lord said in the book of Acts, chapter three verse nineteen that he wants us to turn away from sin, and sin no more. Turn to God and our sins will be wiped away. Do you think that's something you want to do in this case?"

Daniel didn't hesitate. "Yes, sir. And thank you. I haven't been to church in a very long time, but I've tried to lead a decent life…except for that." He blushed. "Maybe it was God that brought me here, not just my GPS," he chuckled.

—◊—

Relieved, Daniel walked over to the Main Street Diner for a late lunch. As soon as he sat down at a table, Ms. Pat came over with a pot of coffee.

"Hello there! Glad to see you came back." She knew this was the only eatery within walking distance of the inn, and didn't see his motorized scooter outside, but gave him her standard greeting anyway.

Daniel smiled. "Glad to be back. I see you have spaghetti and meatballs on special today. I'll have a plate of that please, along with a side salad and Coke."

"Coming right up." Ms. Pat walked over to the waitress and let her know what Daniel wanted. The waitress wrote it up and placed it in the kitchen window and rang the bell.

The diner wasn't packed; the lunch crowd had mostly gone home. There were a just a few patrons in the dining room, mostly locals. One in particular caught his attention, a pretty woman about his age wearing a skirt suit. That wasn't something you saw every day out in the country.

"I hear they've got two guests now. That's one of them," Daniel heard in a stage whisper from one of the patrons. "Not sure how they'll keep them though with all the hammering and sawing."

"Sure, sure. Susan said Harvey told her there was a lot of rot."

Daniel's recollection of the letter nestled amid the garden shed's dilapidation evoked a sense of intrigue, its origins and intended recipient cloaked in uncertainty. As he contemplated the possibility of unearthing additional mysteries during the renovations, a palpable sense of anticipation tinged the air, leaving him eager for what secrets might be revealed.

"Where are they getting the money to fix the place up? It'll cost a pretty penny..."

"I never really minded the tourists that came through, but the world has changed a lot. Who knows what kind of people they'll get now..."

Ms. Pat came over with the coffee pot, even though Daniel hadn't even had time to take a sip, shielding him from the gossipers with her body. "Here, have some coffee," she said loudly. When she saw him glance at the suited woman, she added more quietly, "That's Miss Avery Thompson. She grew up here and went away to college, just like Emma. She's been back a while now though. She wants to build some kind of development, I'm not sure what. She's always over at the mayor's office and permit department.

"She and Emma were friends in junior high but were nothing alike. Emma was at the library a lot, studying her architecture, but that one there was out gallavantin' most of the time. She's smart all right, but too city for me." She gave a wink and walked away.

Daniel's eyebrows rose but he said nothing. Building a development would surely ruin the picturesque valley, whether it was for residential or commercial use. He wondered if Emma knew about Avery Thompson's plans.

—◊◊◊—

Daniel looked up when he thought his lunch had arrived but instead, before him stood Avery Thompson. She gestured to the empty seat across from him. "May I?"

Not knowing what to say at the sudden surprise appearance, Daniel gallantly held out his hand to indicate she should take a seat while he half-stood to acknowledge her presence.

"Are you a guest at the inn?" Avery Thompson inquired, extending a welcoming hand. "I'm Avery Thompson. I'm a native of this town, and I have ambitious plans to modernize it, beginning with the installation of cell towers. You must have noticed the poor internet signal around here," she chuckled. Daniel had to admit, her smile was a bit dazzling. She had an energy about her...*charismatic*, he would call it. She almost seemed like a politician.

"Hello, Avery, I'm Daniel. Yes, I'm staying at the inn and yes, I have noticed the cell signal problem. But won't cell towers destroy the view? Maybe you could bury some fiber optic cables instead?"

Avery flicked her hair over her shoulder and smiled coyly. "Not to worry. Cell towers can be disguised as trees now; they won't even be noticed." She leaned in, her hands clasped in front of her on the table, manicured red nail polish glistening. "But tell me, what are the plans for the inn? I heard it was under construction. Emma got her permits just before I tried to get mine, and the city council will only allow one major project at a time, something about the town's bylaws, blah, blah, blah." She fluttered her eyelashes; an old trick but one that usually works.

Daniel noticed the flutter of eyelashes, a familiar gesture from Izzy's repertoire of manipulative tactics. Having witnessed her maneuvers countless times before, he had become adept at deciphering her subtle movements.

Guardedly, he replied, "I'm not sure of all the plans for the inn, just that I'm doing my artwork out in the garden shed where it's quiet. There is a bit of water damage under windows and some creaking floors, etcetera. We had some contractors come through to give quotes." *We?* When did the Turners and he become we?

"Yes, Yes, I'm sure it will turn out gorgeous," she nodded, a warm smile playing on her lips. "Well, I've got to run. Hope to see you again soon, Daniel." As she extended her hand for a shake upon rising, he mirrored the gesture, their eyes meeting with a lingering intensity. Sensing an opportunity for further insight, she maintained the contact a tad longer than necessary, knowing she'd unravel more of his secrets gradually, like unraveling a spool of thread. Fueled by ambition, she understood the importance of staying informed about her adversaries' actions, crucial for crafting a strategic blueprint to elevate this provincial town into a vibrant 'city away from the city'.

CHAPTER 7

LAUGHTER IN THE WILDERNESS

When Daniel disclosed to Izzy that he had confessed his past relationship with her to the Turners, her reaction was explosive. Losing her leverage over him, she could no longer manipulate him into returning to the city with her using the threat of blackmail. With swift determination, Izzy hastily packed her belongings, delivering a final warning to Daniel before storming out. "This isn't over, Daniel. I brought you to fame and you owe me. I won't simply let you slip away." Although her words sent a chill down Daniel's spine, he tried to brush off the unease as Izzy jumped into her car, slamming the door shut. The engine roared to life, and as she sped away, the gravel scattered in her wake, a tangible echo of her departing fury.

Heads turned and people stopped in their tracks when the Dodge Charger roared out of town just after lunchtime. Ms. Pat watched it speed past the diner with relief. Evelyn Miller heard it through the heavy library door, shaking her head with a quiet tsk-tsk. Gus looked up from the 1978 Ford engine he was working on and watched as it sped out of sight, rounding the corner a little too quickly, leaving a bit of rubber. He gave out a chuckle, remembering how he'd done pretty much the same thing back in the day.

That night after supper, Reverend Samuel and his two daughters headed to the front porch for a bit of relaxation in the rocking chairs. When they got there, they found Daniel lounging on the porch swing.

Daniel quickly jumped to his feet. "I'm so sorry, I didn't know this was the family porch. I'll head upstairs to my room now."

"Sit, sit," said the reverend with a smile. "This is the inn's porch. In fact, it's nice to see someone taking advantage of the warmer than usual weather."

"Climate change," Olivia said half under her breath. Emma gave her a light pinch.

"Yes, Daniel, feel free to stay. There are plenty of chairs. More chairs than guests." She wished she hadn't said that part. It might make her sound desperate. Um, make *them* sound desperate... for guests...

She shook her head and smiled to herself. What kind of ninny would I have to be to have a relationship so soon, and with a guest? Then she laughed aloud. *Ninny?*

Her father looked at her questioningly, but she just shook her head and sat in a rocker, turning a slight pink shade.

Olivia sat on a cushioned bench with her legs tucked up under her while her father took another rocker. Daniel sat back down on the porch swing.

"So," began Reverend Sam, "how did the rest of your day go?" He knew it had to have been tough, what with Izzy storming out the way she did. Daniel must have had some sort of interaction with her that she found displeasing. But the reverend knew not to push it; if Daniel wanted to talk about it, he'd talk about it.

"It was relaxing... after lunch."

The reverend smiled and Emma did too. She couldn't help feeling relieved that Izzy was gone. She'd miss the income another guest would have brought in, but maybe she could pick up a gig on Freelancer.com or something to make up the difference. Once they got the internet situation squared away.

Olivia had been left out of most of the situation. She'd felt the tension at breakfast but wasn't privy to the reason for it. All being well that ended well, she was ready to move on to more interesting topics.

"So, Daniel, we know you have breakfast here and probably lunch at the diner. But where do you go for dinner?" she asked out of curiosity.

"Well, I hope it's not against any rules, but I have a loaf of bread and some peanut butter and marshmallow in my room. I also have some trail mix and bottles of water."

Emma was surprised she hadn't thought to ask the same thing. She sat up a little straighter in her chair. It didn't seem right, an inn guest eating camping food alone in their room.

She looked at her dad, a bit of alarm showing on her face. If this got out on social media (again, once the internet situation was resolved), it reflect on the in badly. Plus, admitting it to herself, it would be nice to have Daniel at the dinner table.

The reverend seemed to read Emma's thoughts – or maybe he was playing a bit of matchmaker. "Son, there's no need for that. We eat dinner every night at around six o'clock and you know there's room at the table. We'd love to have you join us." He turned and barely winked at Emma, who again turned pink. Daniel was oblivious to that, but his stomach involuntarily growled at the thought.

Now he turned red, and everyone laughed.

"I'll take that as a yes," said the reverend, chuckling.

"Yes, and I thank you. I can pay extra –"

Emma was about to thank him for the offer, but her father spoke up first. "No need, we have plenty. Don't we, Emma?"

Emma smiled and agreed. "Yes, of course. But when things pick up this summer... that is, if you're still here and we start getting more guests..." She didn't quite know where she was going with this but was thinking about going broke through serving free meals just when she thought they might be getting ahead financially.

Olivia saved the day. "Maybe Daniel can help out in the garden once it gets going as payment for dinner? Hey, maybe we could get all the guests to help, like a working vacation. It's only an acre, but it's a lot for just us. I don't know how Grandma and Grandpa managed it."

"They had me to help them," laughed the reverend, miming picking fruit from trees.

"That's great, Dad! That's the qigong movement called Picking Cherries," laughed Olivia. The reverend looked puzzled.

Olivia explained, "Qigong, which is pronounced 'chee-gong' or 'chee-kung,' is a traditional Chinese practice that combines movement, meditation, and controlled breathing to cultivate and balance the body's vital energy, known as 'qi' or 'chi.' Qigong is often practiced for relaxation, stress reduction, improved flexibility, and overall wellness.

At that, the reverend gave a small bow and a smile while staying seated and was stunned again by his youngest daughter's seemingly endless intelligence on worldly matters.

"Olivia, that could be a great idea," remarked Emma. "We could consider installing some raised beds to simplify the process. And since we're looking to hire a part-time cook, perhaps we could offer them a reduced salary in exchange for the opportunity to educate our paying guests about herbs and cooking with fresh produce. This way we could share a portion of the proceeds from the classes with them to possibly overreach their salary potential."

She was an architect, not a marketer, but since the pandemic, everything had changed, and people were thinking outside the box for ways to earn income.

"Olivia, you're creating a newsletter for past guests, right?"

"Yes. I could totally put that in there."

"Could you set up a Facebook page for the inn?" she asked. "I was thinking we could livestream the gardening process from the beginning, allowing people to follow along. Then, when they arrive for their stay, they can join in the picking and cooking of the produce that's ready to be harvested."

Daniel gazed at Emma with admiration. Where had she conjured up such a brilliant notion? Aware of their financial struggles, he felt grateful for the opportunity to contribute, first as a guest and now potentially by assisting in the garden. The prospect of livestreaming the process and attracting more guests filled him with hope.

Olivia clapped her hands in delight. "Yes! This is going to be so much fun."

No one noticed the tears of joy in the reverend's eyes as he rocked back and forth, so proud of his girls.

—✺—

The next morning, Emma made pancakes and bacon for breakfast. It was easy once the griddle was heated up. She used plant-based milk and baking powder instead of eggs so Olivia could eat them too. Olivia came in to make her own "facon," as she called it. She used banana peels and some kind of soy sauce marinade. Ick! thought Emma, but minded her own bacon.

After breakfast, a team of workers arrived to commence renovations, overseen by Harvey Sheffield, the contractor of choice. As a local renowned for his craftsmanship, Harvey's reputation preceded him. His wife, Susan, served as the school's lunch monitor, and although they lacked children of their own, they occupied their days with diligent work – and occasional gossip. Emma wasn't overly concerned about the latter.

Daniel saw the large diesel truck pull up and the contractor he'd met before got out, along with a younger fellow. As Daniel packed up his brushes and a sandwich to take to the garden shed, they made their way to the back door with heavy steps. He aimed to avoid being in the workers' path, prepared to seek refuge in the town library's reading room if the noise became too disruptive. Daniel looked forward to conversing with Miss Miller, the librarian, who had a knack for spinning captivating tales, often centered around the town's history.

He passed them on the first floor as they came down the hallway from the kitchen.

"Good morning," he greeted them as they squeezed past each other. "I'm just headed out to the shed to do some sketching." Harvey doffed an imaginary cap in greeting. The younger guy just kept moving, barely giving him acknowledgement.

"Sorry to chase you out," said Emma as they faced each other closely in the narrow hallway. "We're going to start at the front of the house and work our way back and up." She pointed upward. "The roof will be last."

"And costliest," Daniel added. He wanted her to know he understood their plight and he was fine with it, only wanting to stay out of the way, and possibly help along the way.

"Yes," she agreed. She felt a little out of breath. Not sure why; they'd only come from the back of the house to the front hallway. She'd have to get out more, hiking some trails or tooling around town on the mopeds. *Tooling?* She shook her head.

Daniel looked at her expectantly. Had he said something wrong? He could see she was a little breathless. Her cheeks were a bit flushed. He felt the warmth of her, they were so close. Was she ill? He took her hand in concern. Maybe she had a fever.

Emma was surprised at the physical touch and took in a breath. She looked up at him in surprise but then quickly blinked and regained her composure.

That's when he saw it. Or did he imagine it? In that one unguarded moment, her eyes spoke volumes. She wasn't ill. She had feelings for him the same way he was developing feelings for her.

They laughed it off as she pulled her hand from his. Those smooth hands would be her undoing if she wasn't careful…

—⁓—

Out in the shed, Daniel thought about Emma. Surely it was not a good idea to begin a relationship with the proprietor – the reverend's daughter – especially with the tire tracks from Izzy's Charger barely cooled.

He decided to put it out of his mind for now but keep aware of potential tempting situations where Emma was concerned. No more squeezing together in tight hallways.

He brought out his charcoal and stared at the blank easel. He didn't feel particularly inspired, but his art was as much an outlet for his emotions as it was sought after by lovers of his work. He looked at the piece of charcoal in his hand and wondered how working in a garden would affect his ability to draw or paint. It was all becoming much too complicated.

He started by just drawing an arched line across the paper, starting in the lower left and ending in the upper right. Like a writer, just having something on the paper would likely lead to something else.

He gazed out the window, and an image came to his mind. He felt it quite strongly and knew what his subject was to be. He made that diagonal arch the background and began working on the main image.

—⁓—

The diner was hopping, being the main eatery in town. Miss Pat was playing hostess as Daniel arrived. "Well hello there, young man," she greeted. "We're pretty busy today. Would you mind sitting at the counter?"

"Not at all," Daniel replied, following her to the 1950s-style red-and-white counter and round stools, the milkshake machine featured prominently near the cook's order window. "I'll make it easy for you and take the special for today. I know it will be good."

"You got that right!" Miss Pat answered. She just called through the window, "One special!" and headed back toward the door to seat more diners.

Daniel looked at the reflection in the mirror in front of him and saw Harvey Sheffield come in with his young worker in tow. Miss Pat directed them to the counter as well.

Harvey sat a few seats down from Daniel, the young man trying without much success to get a signal on his cell phone.

"Howdy," greeted Harvey, doffing his invisible hat again.

"Hello," replied Daniel. "Break time, I see."

"Yup. We got a good amount of work done this morning. Washed the front porch to get it ready for paintin' and started pulling out some plaster below some windows in the parlor. Found a letter in a cubbyhole in the ceiling of one of the closets."

"A letter?" he had Daniel's full attention now. "What kind of letter?"

"Looked kinda old. Miss Emma was pretty excited about it."

"Was it addressed to anyone?" Daniel asked.

"It had some fancy writin' on the front, somethin' like, *To My One and Only*. Miss Emma didn't open it, just put it in her folder."

The waitress came up to Harvey. "I'll have the turkey club and a cup of the soup of the day," he said before she could even ask. "Same for him." The young man looked up from his phone momentarily, then back down again.

"You know," Harvey addressed Daniel, "a lot of old glass bottles and things are found in walls during renovations, sometimes worth some good money. They're left there by the workers who built the building…usually empty booze bottles," he chuckled.

Daniel couldn't quite understand how Harvey could be so nonchalant about the letter. Then again, he must find old relics in his renovations all the time. But to Daniel, this was becoming a real mystery.

—◊◊—

That night at dinner, Emma showed everyone the letter Harvey had found in the parlor closet. "This is on the same kind of paper and in the same kind of envelope as the one we found in the garden shed," she noted as the letter was passed around. "With the same handwriting. It says *To My One and Only.*"

Olivia began to read.

You are my delight. I think about you day and night.

"It's kind of like a poem," she said. "Not very good," she snickered under her breath. "If the handwriting wasn't so fancy, I might think this was done by a kid."

"It is pretty straightforward," the reverend agreed. "The person obviously loves whomever they're writing to."

The letter made it around to Daniel. "Yes, it does look like the same paper and writing. Maybe the builders left it? Harvey mentioned they leave things behind all the time." He left out the fact that it was often empty liquor bottles. "Do you know who built this house?"

"Yes, it was my great-great-grandfather," said Emma.

"He was the first Turner to arrive here," added the reverend. "He built this house and a small church where our present church stands today. I guess you could say I come from a line of pastors. I'm not sure where he met my great-grandmother, if she was already here or came later. I probably should know more about my own family history."

Daniel immediately thought of Evelyn Miller. "Next time I go to the library, I can ask Miss Miller if there are any family trees or other information about the building of the inn and church."

"That's a great idea," said Olivia. "And I can add that to the newsletter and Facebook page. And maybe some of the other social media channels and apps to see if there are people who know anything about that time in history here... you know how people come and go through here."

Olivia's internet savvy made Emma feel old. The reverend had a sort of blank look on his face, then just nodded and took a sip of his after-dinner coffee.

—⁂—

The crunching of tires in the driveway drew the attention of those inside the house as well as Daniel in the shed. The workers had arrived an hour before and no more guests were expected. Daniel was a bit worried it might be Izzy returning but in fact, it was a pristine Porsche 911, a new model, by the looks of it.

Out stepped a dapper young man dressed to the nines in a tailored Armani suit. He took a look around, eyes lingering on the old inn and Harvey's pickup truck. He shook his head and shut the car door, making his way to the front of the inn.

"Mornin'," greeted Harvey. The gentleman ignored him and began walking up the front steps. He reached for the old-fashioned pull doorbell. "I wouldn't do that if I —"

The man scoffed and grabbed hold of the brass ring pull. He immediately realized his mistake as he withdrew his hand to find it covered in brass polish. He took off his aviator sunglasses with his other hand and glared at Harvey.

"I tried to warn you." Harvey doffed his invisible cap and turned away, making eye contact with the young worker painting the ceiling a lovely shade of light blue. They both tried to contain their laughter but found they couldn't. The man just glared at them, then turned away, dismissing them..

From the upstairs window where Emma was cleaning rooms, she saw her ex-boyfriend pull up and walk up the steps onto the porch. She clutched the pillow she was plumping to her chest and closed her eyes. "No, no, no…" Her legs were turning to jelly at the sight of him, and not in a good way. She'd paid for countless hours of online therapy to bring herself out of the depths of depression when she'd finally found the courage to break things off with Byron Monroe. Now she was back to being a quivering jellyfish.

When she didn't hear a knock or the doorbell, she made her way downstairs to find out what was going on. She could see his silhouette through the stained-glass window on the front door. Was he talking to Harvey? Not likely. Byron was a total snob and wouldn't lower himself to speak with a tradesman.

She reached the front door and opened it to find Byron with his hand out. It was covered in a beige paste of some sort. She looked at Harvey, who glanced over his shoulder at her with a slight smirk. She followed his eyes to the bottle of Brasso on the porch railing.

Her hand flew to her mouth to stifle her own laughter. Byron now turned his glare to her.

"Some kind of welcome," he said, tucking his sunglasses into his suit pocket. He snatched the pillowcase she was holding and used it to wipe the cleaner off his hand.

"Hey!" She tried to grab the pillowcase back from him but it was too late, it was ruined. "Byron, what are you doing here?"

"Sweetie, that tone doesn't suit you. Let's try again, shall we?"

Emma fumed, sweat forming under her arms. He was doing it again, already, trying to control her. Finding fault with everything she said or did. She prayed Byron would be put off quickly by the inn and leave. At any rate, she needed to get that internet connection pronto and possibly continue her online therapy again.

Still, she smiled and asked pleasantly, "Byron, what are you doing here?" *How does he do that?*

"Well, sweetness, I have an event and I need my beautiful girl to dazzle some people for me. I know you've probably realized your mistake by now and want to get away from this" – he waved his hand around the half-painted porch and sawhorses on the front lawn – "construction zone. Why don't we go inside and discuss this?"

Harvey was observing this exchange and already didn't like the fellow. Who does he think he is? He'd have to give Susan an update on this turn of events.

—∿—

"Woohoo!" shouted Olivia. "I got one!" She turned around and put her hands over her mouth at the site of Evelyn Miller looking at her over the tops of her glasses, trying to look stern about the noise but happy to see Olivia back in the library, all grown up now.

"Sorry, Miss Miller."

Evelyn chuckled and smiled, putting Olivia at ease.

"What did you get?" whispered Daniel. He had been next to the computer station in the reading area and heard Olivia's outburst.

"I got us a new guest," she whispered back, barely using her library voice. "I did a Facebook Live where I walked the grounds and talked about the garden-for-dinner plan, and somebody responded! A Liam Thompson," she noted, looking at his profile. "Hmm, he's pretty cute too! Ooh, he has #OccupyWallStreet on his profile."

Miss Miller cleared her throat and Olivia whispered,

"He says he has 'connections in the area' and would like to come for a stay this weekend. I hope Emma doesn't mind, with the renovations still going on. It's only for the weekend," she said hopefully.

"There's only one way to find out," said Daniel. "With hardly any cell service there's no sense trying to call. Let's hop on the mopeds and head back to the inn, if you're done here."

"Yes, I'm finished for the day. I've got all kinds of images and videos on social media. Maybe I should have checked with Emma first. She might get mad if a lot of people start showing up now."

"I can't imagine your sister angry," Daniel said.

Olivia just looked at him. That sounded like something someone in love would say.

Byron Monroe was already gone by the time Daniel and Olivia returned from the library. Harvey and his helper were gone as well. Emma was just coming around the garden path toward the house, out of breath and slightly disheveled. Had she been jogging?

"Hey," said Olivia as she and Daniel dismounted their mopeds and wheeled them into the garage. "I've got some good..." Olivia paused as she took notice of her sister's demeanor. "News." She took in the whole image of her sister as she got closer. "Are you all right?"

Emma just shook her head, her ponytail swinging. She took in a deep breath and slowly let it out. "I'm better. I've been better. I'm fine."

Daniel and Olivia looked at each other, growing concerned at Emma's discombobulation.

"Byron," was all Emma said to Olivia, then turned and walked into the house.

"Uh-oh," said Olivia. "I'd better go in and... help with dinner."

"Sure," said Daniel. "I'll just go to my room. Call me if you need me." He was growing close to this family and had feelings for Emma, but it was not his place to pry. He would say a prayer for her upstairs. That was unlike him to think about praying. This place and these wonderful people were evidently a good influence on him.

In the kitchen, Emma washed her hands and splashed water on her face, finding solace in the familiar feel of her grandmother's dishtowel, a tangible connection to her sage advice. As she dried her face, memories of her grandmother's wisdom flooded her mind. Emma longed for her guidance, remembering the comforting words of Proverbs 15:22, "Plans fail for lack of counsel, but with many advisers, they succeed."

She turned around to face Olivia, leaning against the kitchen sink. "Byron was here today. He wants me to go to some event with him and dazzle his clients again. I sort of told him no."

"You sort of told him no? Does that mean you told him yes? That rat has no right to barge in here on you. You don't have to go with him, you know."

"I know. It's hard to say no to him. It's like… it's like being brainwashed, or drunk. I feel like I have no control."

"And that's precisely why I'm so proud that you left him. He was SO not good for you sis. Mentally and emotionally."

Her sister was right. Emma knew it. She'd have to lean on her for strength, even though she was the older sister and supposedly knew better about these things.

"You're right, and thank you. If Grandma was here, she'd say the same thing. How did you get so wise?" Emma smiled for the first time that afternoon as she reached out and rubbed her sister's arm.

"Aw, go on," said Olivia. "No, really, go on…" They both laughed.

"Oh, I've got good news!" Olivia said, hoping to put a positive spin on Liam's impending arrival. She did not want her sister any more upset than she already was. "How would you like a paying guest this coming weekend? Cha-ching! Cha-ching!"

"This weekend?" Emma looked worried. "But the construction –"

"I don't think that matters to this guy. He's interested in the gardening for dinner I wrote about on social media. I did a Facebook Live tour of the gardens and he wants to check it out. He says he has connections here in the area. Not sure what that means.

"I checked out his profile and he seems outdoorsy, easygoing. We could give him the room what's-her-name just vacated." Olivia still didn't know the details of why Izzy had left, but she knew the tension was gone from the breakfast table and that was good enough for her.

"Yes, we could do that. But let's not invite him to dinner. He'll just be here for the weekend, and we don't want to start that trend."

"And maybe he belongs to a Meetup group that likes to do things together," Oliva added. This summer we could really be slammed with paying guests!"

"We'll need more pillowcases," Emma mumbled, confusing Olivia. But Emma turned and left so Olivia let it go.

—m—

Liam Thompson did arrive for the weekend. He was young, and happy; a real breath of fresh air. Olivia was immediately drawn to him. Not in a romantic way, she told herself, just a fun, cheerful, friendly kind of way. She liked happy people that were heading towards a purpose. She was always trying to learn and meet new people. Proverb 27:17 came to her mind. "As iron sharpens iron, so one person sharpens another."

"These are obviously the gardens," she said to him as they took a walking tour after he'd checked in. "We'll be getting ready to start seedlings in a couple of weeks. Emma wants to build raised beds too, so people of any age or ability can do the garden-for-food thing."

Liam smiled as he looked around. "Yeah, you could widen the paths so wheelchairs will fit. You'll need to build a ramp to one of the inn's doors. I know you're grandfathered in, but adhering to as many of the ADA's requirements is a good thing."

Olivia nodded, seeing a way she could help Emma with the planning of the renovations and bringing revenue to the inn. Her sister was looking a bit unfocused since Byron's visit. This could be just the thing to bring a smile to her face

"I can find some plans online for the boxes, a compost bin, things like that. I guess we could add it on to the house renovations. More money, but like the boomers say, it takes money to make money."

"Nah, we can do that on our own. I was a Boy Scout, I can surely build a box on stilts for raised beds and throw a little pea stone on a path. Maybe for a discount on my room and board?"

Olivia liked that idea, but she'd have to run it by Emma. "I can ask.

I know money can be a hang-up for some people, but it also makes the world go 'round, right?"

"Right, but I like to barter whenever I can. We can leave it open right now and talk about it more over the next couple of weeks. That's when you want to start the garden seedlings, right?"

Wow, he was really gung-ho! "Right."

"So I'll just come back the next few weekends for boxes and pea stone. You'll need a cameraman for your Facebook Live posts anyway. I'd love to see this inn really hopping with young people. Being in the city isn't healthy. Being in nature is where it's at."

Olivia was overjoyed and seriously impressed. Finally, someone with some passion!

CHAPTER 8:

TENSIONS RISE

*O*ne, two, three, four, five... Emma counted in her head to keep herself from exploding. Before her stood Harvey and his earbud-wearing sidekick, Harvey nearly wringing his hands in distress and the kid gazing off and bopping his head to some bass so loud it could be heard by those standing nearby.

"I'm so sorry, Miss Emma. The lumber and nails just haven't arrived. 'Supply chain issues' is what they said, whatever that means."

"Okay, so where do we stand right now?"

"Well, the porch is nearly done. We polished what we could polish and painted what we could paint. Oh, and we found this under one of the floorboards near the brick steps." He handed her a cookie tin. "There's another one of them letters inside."

Emma was dumbstruck. Another letter? She'd have to start a file on these if they found many more.

"The wrought-iron handrails on the stairs have been sanded and coated with black enamel," Harvey continued. "Those holes at ground level can be covered with lattice; I know there's some at the local hardware store here in town." He knew a little about curbside appeal and Emma's wish to start the renovations from the front to the back and then go up.

He continued. "The soft spot in the parlor closet ceiling where we found the letter is an open hole, but you can just shut the door for now and no one will see it."

She nodded, making little circles next to items on her to-do list that were in process but not complete. Her list was woefully lacking in checkmarks.

"Okay, so what about this entryway? We had talked about stripping the wallpaper and sanding and polishing the floors and stairway. Olivia is getting responses from her social media posts about guests wanting to come in sooner rather than later. We may have to start taking some shortcuts."

"Yes, Miss Emma. Usually, changes cost money, as they say. But if you want to just clean and paint over everything in the front hallway, including the stairs, it will make it look nice right away and will be cheaper than sanding down to the natural wood."

Emma didn't like that idea. Part of the charm of the inn was its beautiful maple hardwood flooring. "I'll have to talk that over with Dad," she sighed. Her father had asked her to come to the rescue of the inn, not steamroll over everything. She wanted to honor him by running major ideas by him first before taking action.

"We can leave the rest of the first floor as is for now. No one will be seeing the kitchen...oh, that's not true. Olivia put something on her posts about gardening and cooking. Guests will be in the kitchen."

"You said you wanted us to put new cabinets in there and you were getting new appliances, isn't that right?" Harvey asked.

"Yes," replied Emma, but there's no time for that now. What do you suggest?"

"Maybe we could consider painting them instead of going for a full replacement, at least for the time being," he suggested, feeling a twinge of regret for his honesty as a tradesman. Every time he spoke up, it seemed like money slipped through his fingers. Fortunately, his wife hadn't already allocated the earnings he hoped to make from this job. Chuckling at his own jest, he couldn't help but admire his wife's wisdom and resourcefulness, likening her to the exemplary wife depicted in Proverbs 31:10–31 – truly an excellent partner.

"That's a great idea, Harvey. And don't worry, next year during our slow season, we'll catch up on all these renovations we had planned." She was starting to sweat a little. In the architecture field, changes were common, but mostly in the drafting stage. Things were usually pretty solid by the time it came to actually building something.

"And what about the guest rooms?" she asked. "Guests might not notice paint over wallpaper just coming in and out through the entryway, but they'll notice it sitting in their rooms at night. That wouldn't be good."

Harvey scratched his head. "Let me look into that. I'll probably have to go into the city and check out the big box stores. You and I both would rather use someone local for supplies, and it'll surely cost more money, but at least we can get something decent and quick, if not cheap. You know what they say, you may want cheap, fast, and good, but you can only pick two."

Emma smiled slightly at that. Good old Harvey. She was glad now she'd chosen him as her contractor for the inn's reservations, even if everything that went on was being spread around town by his wife. They were not malicious, they just liked to talk...a lot...about everyone...and everything.

"Okay, maybe check into some faux shiplap or something like that, and get a quote for at least two rooms. Maybe we can do two at a time to speed things up."

"Sure thing, Miss Emma. There's also the option of skim-coating with some spackle and painting, but that will be messy and take more time." Time was money, but that was also a lot of work, and Bopping Boy over there had a lot of muscle but not a lot of skill.

Emma appreciated Harvey's honesty. "Harvey, you're doing a great job. I'm so glad you're here."

Harvey actually blushed a bit and humbly doffed his imaginary hat to her.

"Let me know what you find in the city and when you want to start in the kitchen. We'll need to have a work-around in case it takes longer than expected." She knew it would.

—⁂—

Emma was marching around the garden paths again, trying to lessen the tension she was feeling from the renovation setbacks.

Miss Dot had found time for Emma in her dad's schedule and Emma had told him about the lumber not being available. She felt a little whiny when explaining Olivia had posted on social media and the responses were coming in sooner than expected.

"That's a good thing, right?" he'd asked.

"Well, yes... but –"

"You did ask Olivia to do that, right?"

She took a steadying breath. "Yes."

"I'm sure it will all work out." The reverend smiled and looked at her expectantly. "Anything else?"

Emma shook her head. "No, not really. Thanks, Dad."

Reverend Samuel paused and looked at his daughter. Yes, there was something else. He wasn't sure, but expected it had something to do with her ex-boyfriend's quick visit. And maybe the young artist they had staying with them – he hoped.

"Okay then, I'll see you at dinner?" He stood up and rubbed her shoulder. "You're doing a great job, Emma. I thank you from the bottom of my heart for dropping everything and coming back to help me run the inn."

Emma had slight tears in her eyes. When her daddy was proud of her she was five years old again, learning to ride a bicycle without training wheels. She smiled for real this time. "I'm glad I'm here too, Dad. See you at dinner."

So her marching the paths wasn't so much about the renovations after all. She guessed it took being out in nature to figure things out. Her stress wasn't so much about Olivia anymore either. She had, in fact, asked Olivia to make those posts. And Olivia was helping out tremendously by making most of the dinners. So what was it?

She rounded a corner and the garden shed came into sight. Her heart leapt in her chest a bit, butterflies in her stomach. "No," she said aloud. "It's too soon. I hardly know the man."

She thought about the quick visit by Byron, her ex-boyfriend from the city. It had brought into sharper focus the contrast between a good man and a not-so-good one. Still, she would not allow these feelings to grow. It was unprofessional and also, she didn't have time right now. She needed to get the inn back on its feet – and be really sure she was over Byron-and get her head straight, have some time for herself before embarking on another romantic adventure.

Daniel stepped out of the garden shed just as she was passing. Is he doing that on purpose? She wondered. He was rubbing his hands together and stretching his fingers back. She looked at him quizzically.

"Break time. Just stretching my fingers after gripping the pencil for so long."

"Oh, then you're making progress?

"Yes, I felt inspired and it's going well."

"That's good." They fell into step together, heading back toward the house.

"So," Daniel began, "I saw a pretty fancy car out here the other day. A potential new guest?"

"Um, no, not exactly," Emma replied. She really didn't want to get into a personal story with Daniel, a guest. But he'd been honest with her about Izzy being his ex-girlfriend. And he'd said his honesty had to do mostly with his respect for her father. Reverend Samuel also being a minister probably had something to do with it.

Daniel glanced sideways at her. He could tell she was uncomfortable and didn't want to press the issue. At the same time, he had come clean about Izzy. Maybe he was taking too much for granted about open communication in their relationship. Did they even have a relationship beyond innkeeper and guest? He involuntarily shrugged.

The silence was getting awkward. Emma knew she'd have to say something, if for no other reason than to make a guest feel comfortable.

"No," she said. "That wasn't a potential guest, it was my ex-boyfriend. He came to ask me out."

Daniel's eyebrows raised so high they almost disappeared into his hairline. "Really? What are the chances that both our exes found us in the span of a week?"

She stopped and turned to him. She hadn't thought of that. They had that in common, for sure.

"Yes, it does seem odd, now that I think of it." She looked up at the gray sky. Spring had not quite arrived and everything looked as bleak as she felt. "Do you think we're being tested?"

"Tested? By whom?"

"By God."

"No, my God doesn't test me," he said flatly.

She shook her head in confusion. "What does that mean?"

"It means that God loves us. He's not a mean God that tests us by putting hardship in our paths." His voice was soft, but with conviction. It seemed he'd retained something from vacation Bible school after all.

"God isn't mean when he tests us. But he is a jealous God, it says that right in the first commandment."

Daniel was a bit perplexed. He knew about a woman's jealousy; Izzy had shown that many times during their relationship. But in the end she was only jealous someone would take away her goose that laid the golden eggs. She was only interested in his ability to make her money.

"I don't know about that," Daniel replied. "You're the daughter of a preacher so you'd know best. But isn't jealousy one of the seven deadly sins?"

"What kind of church did you grow up in?" she asked. "Are you Catholic?"

"Well, no, I'm not anything. My mom took me to church as a youngster but it didn't really have a denomination, like Catholic or Protestant. It was just…church."

"Hmm," said Emma, not sure she wanted to have this conversation. She knew good manners suggested not talking about politics or religion, and after all, this was a paying guest. But she was always eager to be a witness and share the goodness of the word. She decided to tread lightly.

"I guess it doesn't matter. They're both exes, and we don't have to worry about them anymore."

Hopefully?…

—m—

Liam did come back the next weekend. The discussion over breakfast moved to the restoration project being on hold due to supply issues.

"I might be able to help with that," he said. "A friend of mine has a homestead. He supplies trees to a lumberyard, a small operation. It's mostly pine, but some oak too. I could ask him if he has any suggestions."

"That would be great!" Olivia said with enthusiasm. She wasn't one to hide her feelings, and this guy was mighty impressive. She smiled a dazzling smile at him and he just smiled back and took a bite of his muffin with gusto.

Emma spoke up, "That reminds me. In all this hubbub, I forgot to tell you all; Harvey found another letter, this one under a porch floorboard near the brick stairs. It was preserved in an old cookie tin."

Daniel's eyebrows shot up in surprise. "Another letter? What does it say?"

"In all honesty, I've been so busy, I haven't even looked. It's up in Dad's office, I'll go get it." Emma excused herself and walked quickly toward the office.

"Letter?" Liam asked. Olivia filled him in on the two mysterious letters they'd found already, one in the shed, the other in the parlor closet ceiling.

"We think they may have been left by the builders. They're kind of like love letters or poems."

"Cool!" said Liam. "Maybe you can put that in the newsletter too, draw a crowd of online sleuths."

The reverend was looking a bit worried. "How about if we wait on that and just see what the letters say? We don't want to have a stampede of people thinking the inn is haunted or anything; that would be misleading." As it states in Romans chapter twelve verse twenty-one: 'Do not be overcome by evil, but overcome evil with good.'"

Daniel was glad Reverend Turner said that. He was beginning to get the creeps thinking things were buried in the walls. Literal skeletons in closets? He involuntarily shivered.

Emma came back with the tin. "It's hardly even rusted; whoever put it there knew what they were doing."

She opened the lid and took out the letter, handing it to her father. "*To My Heart's Desire,*" he read. He opened the letter carefully. "*You are my delight. My steps shall not slip.*"

Blank faces stared back at him. "What does that even mean?" Emma finally asked. "Is it a blessing on the brick stairs?"

Something triggered in the reverend's mind. *Delight... steps shall not slip...* He started to nod. "Let me get back to you on this." He rose from his chair and everyone else did too. "Have a great day, all." He made his way out the door, heading to his church office.

—◊—

Later, at the diner, Liam, Olivia, and Daniel were seated at a table having lunch. Emma said she was too busy, so they planned to bring her back a chef salad.

Harvey walked in and ambled up to the counter nearby, Harvey doffing his invisible cap at Olivia on his way by. His apprentice had taken the day off with the slowdown in work.

"Harvey, why don't you sit with us?" Olivia said, waving to a chair. "I want you to meet someone."

Harvey came over and took a seat.

"Harvey, this is Liam. He's staying with us at the inn on weekends and thinks he can find some lumber for the restoration."

Harvey held out his hand and Liam shook it. "Hello, son. How have you been?"

Olivia was confused. "You two know each other?"

"Sure," said Harvey. "You're probably too young to remember –"

Just then, the waitress came over to take their orders. A garden salad with white beans on it for Olivia (no, they did not have tofu), pasta marinara for Liam, and a burger and fries for Daniel. Harvey was getting two turkey clubs to go. They'd order Emma's salad just before leaving.

"Remember what?" Olivia continued the conversation.

"Liam is –"

Avery Thompson came bustling in. She had seen Liam sitting at the table and needed to find out what was going on. She decided on her strategy right then and there.

"Daniel, how nice to see you," she nearly purred as she got too close to the table, her hip touching Daniel's arm. He instinctively leaned a bit in the other direction. Avery pulled out another chair and sat down uninvited.

"Harvey," she nodded. Harvey moved to doff his invisible cap, but without much of a smile. Avery was a little troublemaker when she was younger, and his memory was long.

"Liam," she said next, turning her attention to him. "What are you doing here?" She tried to smile, but it was a bit weak.

"I'm staying at the inn for the weekend. How've you been, sis?"

"Sis?" Olivia couldn't help the squeak in her voice.

"Yes," said Harvey. "You probably don't remember him because you were so young when Liam moved to the city with his mum…" Harvey was embarrassed; maybe he shouldn't have brought up that Avery and Liam's parents had divorced. The divorce was ugly, and the entire town was sure to remember the hatred shown between the two. It was a bit of a *Peyton Place* kind of scandal.

The wheels in Olivia's head churned double-time. "Oh, so she's your 'connection' to the area," she said with air quotes around *connection*.

"Yes. I don't come back often, never had the need." He looked at Avery with laughter in his eyes while she silently fumed. He was messing up her attempt at appearing like the perfect type A go-getter entrepreneur. "But now I have a better reason." This was said softly and kindly and with a pleasant and open look to Olivia.

"You do?" Olivia was melting right before their eyes.

"Yes. I'd love to help with the renovations at the inn, if Harvey needs a hand. I'm pretty good with building raised bed gardens and expanding those stone pathways."

"Pretty good?" Avery nearly snorted. She'd have to be more careful to keep up appearances. "If running your own successful hardscaping business is pretty good then yes, he's pretty good."

All eyes turned to Liam.

"What?" he said with a smile.

—⚬—

As if that revelation weren't enough, Byron and Izzy both returned the following weekend; Byron to further press Emma to attend the event with him, Izzy to perform damage control with Daniel and the Turners.

Daniel had hoped she'd just leave him alone, but now knew that wouldn't be the case. He would have to confront the unresolved feelings and complexities of his past with Izzy. The best place to do that was the quiet of the garden shed, so he quickly excused himself and made his way outside.

Without much to do after breakfast with Daniel gone and Emma ensconced in the office – on purpose, to avoid Byron – Byron drove Izzy into town to see what they could see. Emma had made herself scarce, so Reverend Turner offered mopeds to the pair. Byron looked horrified and Izzy bit her lip to keep from screaming out in laughter. *What a bunch of hicks!*

In the first boutique they entered, Byron sneezed and loudly exclaimed, "Eww, so dusty in here!"

Izzy went to a rack and pulled something off it. "Look at this. It looks like something from *The Andy Griffith Show*. Where's Aunt Bea?" she laughed.

The shopkeeper was less than amused as she made her way over to the pair. "Is there something I can help you with?"

"I doubt it," sniffed Byron. "We're just trying to amuse ourselves for a few hours. I have important business to discuss with someone. Otherwise, I wouldn't be caught dead in this... this..."

"Nowhere land," finished Izzy, sniggering. "Do you have any Coach bags or Chanel suits?" she asked, knowing full well there wouldn't be any. "No call for such things around here," replied the shopkeeper. "Most of our clientele work for a living or come here for their Sunday best."

"Sad to hear that," said Byron. "Let's go." He offered Izzy his arm and she took it, both of them turning on their heels and turning up their noses as they exited the store.

Secretly, they both knew they were just put in their place by the shopkeeper, but their egos wiped it from their memory quickly as they continued.

CHAPTER 9

UNVEILING THE PAST

The noise from the renovations did, in fact, become too distracting for Daniel. He headed for the solace of the town library.

He was happy to see Miss Miller there at the desk, cataloguing books.

"Good morning," he said quietly in his library voice. She just nodded and smiled.

Daniel hesitated. Since he hadn't planned on coming here, he was feeling a bit lost. Should he just find something to read, or listen to some music? Hop on a computer and see what's going on in the world? A hard no to that last option. He liked being away from it all. The world would go on without him. He had an idea.

He meandered over to the reception desk. Miss Evelyn noticed and put the book in her hand in a pile and made her way over to Daniel.

"Something I can help you with?" she asked pleasantly. Her smile made it all the way to her bright-blue eyes.

"Yes, Ms. Miller. You seem to know an awful lot about the town and its origins," he began.

She gave a quiet chuckle. "Yes, well, I wasn't actually here at the founding. I'm not *that* old."

Daniel squirmed and blushed. "Oh, I know, I –"

"Daniel, I was just teasing. What is it you want to know?"

"Well, it's about the inn, and the renovations going on. We've found a couple of letters stashed in odd places throughout the house, and even in the garden shed."

Evelyn Miller's eyes lit up. *So, they've found them!* "Yes? And how can I help?"

"You know so much about the founding of the town, I wonder if you have any details about who may have written them and what they mean."

"I may. How many have you found, and what do they say?"

"We've found three; one in the shed, one in the front parlor closet ceiling, and one near the front steps. They seem like love letters or blessings on the house. One is about escaping and prospering, one is in lover's prose, and one we think might be a blessing on the front steps of the inn."

Miss Evelyn smiled at his interpretation. "And what do you want to know?

"Well, do you know who could have put them there? Reverend Turner said his grandfather built the house, but did he build it with his own hands, or did he have a crew come out? It could have been one of the builders; apparently, they're known for leaving relics behind." He decided to omit Harvey's supposition that most of what was left behind was empty booze bottles from workers drinking on the job.

"From what I understand," Miss Evelyn began, "the first Reverend Turner appeared with not much more than the clothes on his back and a horse and wagon. He was one of the first to settle down here rather than just go straight on through heading west. He had a horse and not a mule; that much is noted especially in some of the town's older documents."

Daniel didn't appear impressed.

"That means he was wealthy. Poor people couldn't have afforded a horse and carriage."

Daniel nodded in understanding.

"As you know, the inn was one of the first large buildings built here. The church was built first. Reverend Turner senior must have slept in the church or with neighbors. Maybe he slept in the wagon. The good people of the town would have turned up to raise the church. You've seen the movie *Seven Brides for Seven Brothers?*"

Daniel shook his head no. Miss Evelyn tsk'd. "Maybe check it out on YouTube next time you're here." Daniel nodded.

"I can see the community coming together to build a church. But what about the inn? Would the townspeople have helped with that as well?" he wondered aloud.

"Most likely not," replied Miss Evelyn, letting Daniel come to his own conclusions.

"But if the reverend was wealthy, he could have hired people to build it for him. But why show up with just a horse and wagon? It's almost like he was running from something. Or maybe heading west? The gold rush would have been long over by then." Daniel was more perplexed now than before. "I'm stumped."

"Let me tell you a little story," said the librarian.

This was what Daniel was hoping for.

She started her story as she started most of her stories. "When I was a little girl, my mother told me how her grandmother had died during the influenza pandemic of 1918. It was when soldiers were coming back from World War I. It struck young people the hardest, for some reason."

"Yes, I've heard about that. It came up during the coronavirus pandemic, comparisons to how many died and all that."

"Well, it seems some other young people in town died as well."

Daniel tried to get the conversation back on track. "But what does that have to do with the letters?"

"I'm getting to that," Miss Evelyn said patiently. "The flu was apparently brought in by a young woman who lived here. She had been passing through on a Sunday but after stopping in the church and meeting the first Reverend Turner, she decided to stay. They say, it was love at first sight. The couple were married very soon after."

"Oh, the reverend will be very interested to hear that! He said he didn't know much about his great-grandmother, she was never really mentioned."

"Not surprising," said Miss Evelyn, the smile fading from her eyes. "She died soon after. It was she who brought the influenza to Graceville. The first Reverend Turner built those letters into the house as part of his penance."

—⁂—

Daniel didn't know how to tell the family the news Miss Evelyn had shared. It didn't make sense.

First, how could the current Reverend Turner have been born if his great-grandmother died so soon after marriage? And how could they have known it was she who brought the pandemic to Graceville? They didn't have sophisticated testing like today. Still, it would explain why no one spoke of her.

Daniel decided to tell Olivia the story. The journalist in her would surely be able to get to the bottom of things. That way, his conscience would be clear that he wasn't keeping a secret, and more importantly, he wouldn't bring news that could upset Emma and the reverend.

After a breakfast buffet of what Olivia called morning rice, warm brown rice with plant milk and a variety of fixings like chopped apples, cranberries, and walnuts, Daniel offered to help with the dishes. He followed Olivia into the kitchen.

"Olivia, I spoke with Miss Miller at the library. She had some news about the letters we've been finding."

Olivia looked at him with a smile and eyebrows raised.

"No, it's not good. Seems your great-great-grandmother brought the 1918 flu pandemic to Graceville and some people died, including her. Your great-great-grandfather felt so guilty, he built letters into the walls in some sort of penance.

Olivia's mouth dropped open. "What?!" she yelled.

Daniel shushed her. "Shh! I don't want Emma or your father to be upset until we can determine if that's the truth. Well, if *you* can determine it. You're a journalist, so you'd know how to get to the bottom of a story. I'd start with Miss Evelyn though. There has to be more proof than just her stories. Which are usually delightful," he added, still a bit shocked at the revelation.

"Yes, I'll get to the bottom of this before saying anything to Dad and Emma. Plus, this kind of news could really put a damper on our marketing efforts." She absentmindedly chewed her bottom lip.

"What could put a damper on our marketing efforts?" Emma asked as she brought a tray into the kitchen. "Is something wrong?"

Daniel and Olivia made quick eye contact and then each looked away. Emma felt a little pang of jealousy. *Should I be worried?*

"Well, I've got to run. Charcoal and canvas await," Daniel said, beating a hasty retreat. *Phew! That was close.*

Emma raised her eyebrows at Olivia expectantly.

"What? I've got work to do at the library. I'll be home for dinner. You don't mind washing up since I cooked, do you?" Olivia didn't wait for an answer as she rushed past Emma and up the stairs to grab her things. She was excited at the opportunity to flush out some facts, but worried about what she might find.

—⁕—

Emma was sitting in the office, thinking about those letters. That must be what Daniel and Olivia were talking about. But how could they possibly hurt their marketing efforts?

She shook her head, her mind falling back on Daniel and the jealousy she had felt that he and Olivia shared some secret. Then she remembered James 3:16: "For where jealousy and selfish ambition exist, there will be disorder and every vile practice."

She would work on eradicating it. How, she wasn't sure. She made a note on her pad. 'Get Internet guy out here pronto.' The sooner she could get back to some therapy, the stronger she'd feel. The words came to her, 'the helmet of salvation.' Yes, she'd have to guard her mind against mayhem. 'The breastplate of righteousness.' She'd protect her heart, not from the potential for love, but from jealousy, by staying professional with regard to Daniel but not a statue made of stone. She was grateful for being a pastor's daughter and knowing she wasn't in this alone.

Emma thought about the letters. She wasn't sure in what order they'd been written, but there were some similarities with her and Daniel's meeting and subsequent friendship. He'd come here to escape the city, he'd said. The letter said the person had come here to escape the "ungodly." The second letter mentioned thinking about someone day and night. That was here; thoughts of Daniel would creep in more often than she realized. She'd see something and think, Daniel would love that. Or she'd hear a birdsong and wonder if he was hearing it too, out in the shed. And the third letter, "my steps shall not slip." He had kept her from falling that first day at breakfast when they'd startled each other.

She shook her head to clear it. "Grasping at straws." She should not be in such a hurry to find love again, especially with Byron forcing himself back into her life.

—⁕—

Olivia decided to interview some of the locals under the pretense of the inn's newsletter and social media pages. She also hoped to glean information about the 1918 flu pandemic, and whether her great-great-grandmother could be blamed for bringing it to town.

She stopped first at Gus's gas station. He was a friendly old man, her grandfather's age. He was like a dad or uncle to her own father. They'd been good friends as long as she could remember.

Gus was happy to help. He talked about the town when he was young, how it had grown but still felt like a community. He was a bit stumped when Olivia started asking questions about the flu pandemic, not sure what that had to do with the inn. He didn't know much about it, so shrugged his way through that part of the interview. Olivia made a checkmark next to his name on her pad. He scratched his head as she thanked him and hopped on her moped, heading toward the diner.

Olivia caught Miss Pat at the counter and asked her most of the same questions as she'd asked Gus. Between filling up coffee cups, Miss Pat was happy to answer as many questions as she could about the town, local politics, what it was like when she was a child during the Depression. But when Olivia started asking questions about the flu pandemic of 1918, Miss Pat's lips became like a straight line across the bottom of her face. She'd heard stories, and didn't want to hold it against this generation of Turners. Olivia sensed the change in Miss Pat's demeanor and made a note on her pad. And beside it – a frowny face.

As she made her way through town on her moped heading toward the library, people started buzzing. What was going on at the inn that Olivia would be asking so many questions of the townsfolk? Avery was the most interested of them all.

CHAPTER 10

A GLIMPSE OF REDEMPTION

Emma's persistence with her cell phone carrier paid off, although she did have to finally contact her state legislator for assistance. A cell tower was built on the edge of town.

In fact, it was located at Gus's gas station. "I don't know much about technology," he'd said, "but if it helps the Turners, it's all right by me. They even disguised it as an evergreen. Not sure it'll fool the redtails though."

The signal tower helped more than the Turners. The town was buzzing about the new ease of accessing the internet. Packages began arriving from Apple and Amazon to many households, looking suspiciously the same size as a cell phone or laptop.

Even Avery Thompson, who had initially tried to thwart the effort by proclaiming the dangers of cell signals to the locals, had to admit it would help her in the long run — assuming she was able to get the go-ahead to build her development. She now started envisioning strip malls all the way into and out of town as well.

"I've heard those cell signals cause cancer," she had noted to one diner trying to enjoy their blue plate special. She figured targeting the elderly would get her farther than trying to scare the young people.

"You must be thinking of windmills," she scoffed. The other ladies at her table tittered at her quick response.

Avery blinked hard, shocked at her inability to rattle the woman. She'd have to stick to the men of the town, using her charisma to draw them over to her side. For now, this battle was over.

Daniel walked into the Main Street Diner, surprised by the subtle change. Part of the counter was now occupied by extension cords attached to laptops in front of young people sitting on the stools.

To the right of them, along the side wall, Harvey and his young helper were building a thin counter of about the same height, with electrical outlets underneath that showed both plugs and USB connections.

Harvey looked up and nodded his head at Daniel. "Don't worry, we came in after hours to do most of the work and we're just putting the final screws in now. Ms. Pat wants the counter for eaters. This here is for the internet barroom."

Daniel looked at him quizzically. The young assistant finally spoke. "Cyber café," he explained, trying to not say out loud, "Okay, boomer," but his face said it all.

Avery came sauntering over, hooking her arm through Daniel's. "Well, hello again! You're just in time to join me for lunch."

Harvey's eyebrows shot up almost through his imaginary cap brim. Avery could sway a lot of townsfolk, but Harvey saw right through her – one of the few men in town who did. Maybe because his was such a happy marriage, even childless.

Daniel, not wanting to be rude, simply allowed Avery to lead him to a table. She let go of his arm and stood by her chair expectantly, waiting. Daniel paused a moment, feeling manipulated, but pulled out her chair for her and pushed it back in as she sat down. He then took a seat across the table from her.

"So, big doings up at the inn, huh?" she began. Her aim was to wheedle the inn's plans out of Daniel so she could better plan her own strategy.

"Yes," he began, his eyes discreetly searching the diner for a friendly face to come to his rescue. "Now that the internet signal is stronger, Olivia's marketing efforts will be much easier."

Avery coolly picked up a menu, pretending to peruse it. The diner had been selling the same meals for God only knew how long. "Marketing plans?" she repeated lightly, trying to appear distracted. Her mind began to race. They were getting ahead of her! She had to find out more.

She smiled over the top of her menu. "What will you be having?" she asked sweetly. "Everything looks so good. I think I'll just have a salad though. I've got to watch my figure; after all, swimsuit season will be here before you know it." She sat up straight and arched her back a little. *That ought to get his imagination going.*

It did. Daniel smiled. "You have nothing to worry about." He played right into her hands...

He cleared his throat. "I think I'll just have the grilled cheese and a cup of soup. I love that they make the sandwiches on homemade bread."

"Yes, you must be getting stale muffins and boxes of cereal for breakfast up at the inn." Avery hoped so, anyway.

"Oh, no, the breakfasts are delicious. Emma and Olivia take turns cooking until they can hire some help. Emma makes delicious pancakes and scrambled eggs, and Olivia can cook up some plant-based meals that would *almost* fool a carnivore," he laughed. It was a private joke in the family about Olivia slipping them vegan food every once in a while.

Avery's smile stayed plastered to her face but inwardly she fumed a little. If the inn's business took off, she'd never get her development permits. The townspeople would say one bustling business was enough.

"Yes, well, that's great to hear," she finally managed. *I should win an Oscar for this performance.*

"So, tell me about these marketing plans. The whole town is thrilled about the signal tower going up and the new access to the internet. How is that helping Olivia?"

"Well, Olivia used to have to go to the library to work on the web page and social media accounts, but now she can do that from the inn. And when people request information, she can respond almost immediately instead of just once a day when she is at the library. She can even livestream videos now so potential guests can keep up with what's happening at the inn."

"Why didn't I think of that?" she mumbled to herself. Of course, she could find out everything just by going online and following their internet presence!

"What was that?" Daniel asked, leaning in to hear her better. That was her opening.

She put her menu down and reached out to hold the hand he used to brace himself for his lean-in. He instinctively tried to retrieve it but she held on tight enough that it would snap back if released now.

"Nothing," she said, smiling again, turning off the charm. "I just remembered I have an appointment, er, an errand to run. It was so very nice to see you, Daniel. We'll have to do this again."

She released his hand and stood up from the table, once again looking at him expectantly. He slowly rose from the table in a sign of respect and she smiled, nodded, patted his arm, and took off at almost a power walk, being sure to sway her hips just enough to garner attention from the men, but not enough to invoke the ire of the ladies in the room.

As Daniel returned to his seat, Ms. Pat, who had witnessed everything, just shook her head and made her way over to his table, coffee pot in hand.

Daniel took a moment to compose himself. *What was that all about?* He looked up to see Ms. Pat in front of him, filling his coffee cup without even asking.

"So," she began, not making eye contact. "Looks like Miss Avery has taken a shine to you."

"You think?" Daniel asked. He recovered. "Yes, it was a… pleasant surprise," he said, not sure if he even believed himself.

"Seems a bit odd, since she and Emma were rivals of a sort in high school." She now looked at him squarely. "Avery always wanted whatever Emma had."

Daniel didn't respond, just looked at her expectantly. Miss Pat sighed. She'd have to spell it out.

"So now that Emma has the inn renovations going, and the cell tower, and a handsome, young guest…"

Daniel blushed and looked down at his menu. He could see now where this was going. "Ah, yes, well, I'm very happy at the inn, and the family has been very welcoming."

Some ladies at the next table all but leaned over like they were in an EF Hutton TV commercial. Miss Pat shooed them away with her eyes.

"Yes, I'm sure they have. The town thinks very highly of *these* Turners. Reverend Turner helps all those in need, even if they're not members of his congregation. And the girls losing their mother so young, it just tears at the heart strings. Maybe that's why it would be nice to see them well-matched and settled. There aren't a lot of eligible bachelors in town, ya know." She winked and sauntered off, calling over her shoulder, "Your waitress will be right over."

Daniel pondered her words. True, his feelings for Emma had been growing. He saw her as an efficient, friendly, pretty woman. He knew her being friendly had a lot to do with him being a paying guest. Her efficiency at overseeing the inn's renovations and developing the marketing plan still astounded him.

And pretty? Yes, she was pretty. It was a different kind of pretty, he decided. With Izzy, he was drawn into her whirlwind of a life and before he knew it, he was in her bed.

With Emma, he didn't feel like that. There was no whirlwind, no manipulation – Avery quickly sprang to mind – and no pretense. When they conversed, it was sober and inflective. When they laughed together, it was silly and fun. When he saw that she was worried, or tired, or otherwise discombobulated – like when that Byron came to town – he was concerned for her and wanted to help her feel better.

He reviewed his past relationship with Izzy versus what a future relationship with Emma might look like. There was no comparison. "Lust versus...love?" he mumbled. Luckily, the ladies at the next table had gone back to their lunches.

It was time to go speak with the reverend.

No, it was time to go speak with Emma's father.

—⁂—

Miss Dot greeted Daniel with a cheery hello, then saw the serious expression on his face.

"Hello, Miss Dot. Is there any chance I could speak with Reverend Turner?"

"Of course, of course. He's out right now but he'll be back in"—she looked at the paper calendar on the desk in front of her, sticky notes everywhere—"about fifteen minutes. Would you like to wait?" She gestured to a chair.

"I'll wait, but could I go into the sanctuary?" he asked.

Oh boy, this is serious, thought Dot. "Yes, of course. Right down the hall and up the stairs. I'll let him know you're here when he arrives."

"Thank you," Daniel said, and headed from the office to God's house.

He walked through the door and immediately felt peace. This was an old-style church, with pews instead of chairs. There was an altar in front and a balcony at the back for the choir and organist.

Daniel sidestepped his way to the middle of a pew near the front and sat down. He enjoyed the stillness, and his racing mind and heart immediately slowed.

After a few moment of quiet contemplation, he heard footsteps coming up the stairs and his heart rate sped up again. In walked Reverend Turner.

The reverend walked quietly over to where Daniel sat and took a seat next to him, both men gazing forward.

"It's good to see you here, Daniel," said the reverend. "Is there a special reason for your visit?"

"Yes, Reverend, there is. I've been thinking... I've been very happy in the few months I've been here. I've enjoyed the hospitality from you, your family, and the people in town. It's just that..." He trailed off.

The reverend sat quietly for a moment. He'd dealt with many people who had trouble expressing themselves, whether out of fear, embarrassment, or shame. He drew on his experience as a helper and man of God to help this man sitting beside him, not just Daniel, but one of the Lord's sheep.

"If there's something troubling you, son, you can know that here, I'm Reverend Turner, not your landlord. If you need spiritual guidance, I'm here for you, as a pastor. You've already told me about you and Izzy, and you see the sky didn't come crashing down on us." Using humor usually helped people open up.

"Yes, but, sir, there's something else."

"Oh?"

"Yes, you see, Izzy and I didn't just date, we... we... slept together. We pretty much lived together. I know that's a sin, and just because everyone else is doing it doesn't make it right." Daniel seemed to relax a little after getting that out.

"And the reason you're telling me this is?" the reverend asked the open-ended question.

"Sir, I'm requesting permission to court your daughter."

Silence.

"I realize we're under the same roof and everything, but I can promise you, there'll be no... extraneous behavior of that nature."

It took all the reverend had in him to not burst out into laughter. Joyous laughter, not humiliating laughter. He turned his head toward Daniel, his eyes sparkling.

Daniel turned his eyes to the reverend and saw the happiness on his face. He let out a breath he didn't even know he was holding and smiled. He felt forgiven and clean and all that comes with confessing a sin to a pastor. He also felt a little scared at taking his friendship with Emma to a new level.

The reverend held out his hand and Daniel shook it. His next words were not what Daniel expected to hear.

"Good luck."

—⁂—

At dinner that night, Emma was surprised when Daniel walked in with the reverend – and a bouquet of flowers. The two of them sure did look like they were up to something.

"Hello, Emma. Olivia," said the reverend as they came in the back door through the kitchen. He looked at Daniel. "Olivia, honey, would you help your dad with something before dinner?"

Olivia, glad to be relieved of kitchen duty, jumped at the chance. "Sure, Dad, what is it?"

"It's about the computer in the office. I need your expertise on something. Would you come with me?"

"Absolutely! I mean, Emma, do you need me to do anything else?"

Emma laughed at how transparent Olivia was, but still loved her for it. "Go on, I just have to assemble the salads and make the dressing."

Olivia removed one of her grandma's aprons and tossed it over the back of a chair, following the reverend out. *Did he just wink at Daniel?*

Emma resumed her chopping. Daniel stood there in silence for a few seconds. In all his coming to terms with his past with Izzy and deciding to move forward with Emma, he hadn't actually thought about *how* to go about it.

He cleared his throat and Emma looked at him. He held out the flowers. "Oh, thanks, those will look lovely on the dining room table. Why don't you grab a vase and put them in it?" she said.

"Well, they're not for the table, they're for you," he managed. "I mean, you can put them on the table if you want..."

His changed tone made her turn her head slowly, as if she'd just heard a rattlesnake four feet away and was afraid to move. She looked at him and saw him standing there with the flowers still held out, a – well, goofy would be the only word to use – look on his face.

"What's this all about?" she asked, putting down the knife and accepting the flowers.

"Well, I was thinking today, and I talked it over with the reverend – your father. I really like you, Emma. I've been sort of afraid to say it, what with Izzy coming here and making a scene. And we do have a business arrangement. But I was thinking, you're funny, you're smart, and you're very pretty –"

Her eyes went big and her mouth dropped open. Was he going to propose? No, Dad would never condone that. She shut her mouth. Daniel continued.

"So I was thinking, maybe we could spend more time together, not just as innkeeper and guest, but as... more than that."

"More than that?" she repeated. "What does more than that mean? And you talked to my dad about this? Why?" She began to blush. This was all pretty embarrassing.

This was not going the way he thought it might. He took control of his senses for a moment and became his old self. "Yes, I talked with your dad, for the same reason I told him about Izzy before. Out of respect."

Bad move to bring up the ex, Emma thought. She had been wooed by Byron for about two weeks before he started showering her with gifts and treats and bringing her to fancy, expensive restaurants and other places. He'd swept her off her feet and at the time, she loved it – and thought it was love. But soon enough the real Byron came out and it had taken her countless hours of therapy to get over his mind games. Did she really want to risk that again?

"Daniel –" she began.

"And as for more than that, I just mean I think you're a remarkable woman, and I'd like to get to know you better not as your guest, but as someone special. Emma, I think *you're* someone special. Really special. I'd like us to go on a date."

Emma was relieved in a way. A date was not a proposal. And she'd deal with her father later.

"Daniel, I'm flattered –"

His look of admiration turned into puppy dog eyes in a heartbeat.

She tried again. "Daniel, I'm flattered *and* I think you're special too." She added the end of the sentence on quickly and it worked. No more puppy dog eyes.

"However –"

Puppy dog eyes.

"However," she tried again, "I don't have a lot of free time..."

He started shaking his head. He wasn't buying it.

"What with the renovations and all..."

He was starting to smile and reached out his hand. She took it, and he led her out onto the back porch.

"Daniel, there's something you need to know about me before this continues."

He turned to look at her, a solemn, caring expression on his face. He was really listening to her. *How refreshing.*

"You see, Byron, the man who was here before, he and I were an item in the city." She looked down. "He's not a nice man. He's what they call a narcissist. He'll do anything to keep up appearances in front of others, and he seemed to think I was just the arm candy he needed to get ahead in business and in his social life."

Daniel clenched his jaw but didn't say anything.

"It took me a lot of therapy to understand what was happening. I only knew I was miserable and didn't know why. That's one of the reasons I jumped at the chance to come home and help Dad out with the inn. I needed to distance myself from Byron.

"So, what I'm saying is, I'm not sure I'm ready for another relationship just yet, never mind that you're a guest here and it would be totally inappropriate."

"So what I'm hearing you say is you're afraid I might do the same thing? Mess with your head?" He seemed a little dejected but was trying to stay objective.

"No. No, I don't think that." So, what did she think? What was holding her back? She liked Daniel very much, and in a romantic way too. Here he was saying he felt the same way and wanted to take her on a date. Why was she hesitating?

"What I'm saying is, I'm afraid. I was very hurt, almost broken. Olivia is the only one who knew. Dad doesn't even know. I just feel a bit too fragile."

"Emma, thank you for telling me this. I'm honored that you told me. I can assure you, it won't happen again, not with me, anyway. I respect you, and I admire you." He paused and laughed. "And your father and Olivia – and probably half the town – would kill me, so you have nothing to worry about."

Emma laughed too, and a shiver ran up her arms. It was a shiver of delight, not of fear. She smiled a smile that went all the way to her eyes.

"So is that a yes?" Daniel asked hopefully.

"That's a yes."

CHAPTER 11

CONFRONTING CHALLENGES

W ith the stronger internet signal finally putting Graceville on the map, so to speak, new faces were showing up around town every day. So far, none had been of any concern to the locals, simply curious visitors who may have thought about visiting or staying longer.

One young lady in particular had come to apply for a waitress or cook job at the Main Street Diner. There was something a bit off about her. She didn't have a perky, upbeat, waitress-type personality. She seemed depressed, or perhaps was on anti-depressants. Slightly disheveled, no makeup, hair pulled back in a low ponytail, she never smiled once during the interview and at times looked on the verge of tears.

Ms. Pat didn't quite know what to make of her. She must have been young, judging from the high school graduation date on her resume, but she looked ten years older. She wanted to help the young woman – Tracy was her name – but decided she probably needed more than just a job. She might need to speak with the reverend, or maybe a doctor or therapist, some professional who could really help her.

Ms. Pat thanked her for coming in but said the diner would keep looking. She offered to bring Tracy some pie and coffee before she headed back to the city. Tracy thanked her and sat back in her chair, looking a bit confused. She didn't make eye contact with Ms. Pat when the coffee and pie was set in front of her, just gazed out the window.

Olivia and Liam came into the diner shortly after, taking a break from building the compost bins for the inn's garden. Liam had used the instructions from the *Crockett's Victory Garden* book to make what was called the "Cadillac of composters."

"So tell me again how this works," Olivia said as they sat down.

"There are three bins side by side. You put the scraps in the first bin and keep turning it every few days. When it settles to about half full, you put it into the next bin, then start adding fresh scraps to bin number one. Then when bin number two breaks down to about half its volume, you put it into bin number three, then put bin number one into bin number two, and keep going until the end result is black gold in bin number three..."

Olivia stared at him blankly like he was speaking a foreign language.

"Just trust me, it'll be great," Liam laughed, totally in his element.

His laugh drew Tracy's attention. She finally became a bit animated as she looked at Liam. Ms. Pat watched her and thought her expression was odd. Maybe wistful? There was more to this story than met the eye, of that she was sure.

She stopped by Tracy's table with her ever-present coffee pot. "You came all the way from the city to interview here. Is there anything else you'd like to tell me about why you didn't just take a job near where you live?"

Tracy finally met her eyes. She could sense this woman was kind-hearted, but she wasn't one to just tell everyone her business. Could she trust this stranger? No, she decided. Better to keep herself to herself.

Ms. Pat saw Tracy shut down and just shake her head no, her eyes beginning to well up. Her heart broke for this young woman. "Hon, why don't you bring your plate back to the kitchen? The interview is over, so we're just two people talking now, okay?"

Tracy nodded and stood up, plate in hand. They went back to the kitchen, out of earshot and eyesight of others. The body movement seemed to release something in Tracy and she relaxed a bit.

Ms. Pat took the plate and made gentle eye contact, raising her eyebrows as an indication for Tracy to spill.

"Ms. Pat, I came looking for a job out here because I saw how small and quiet the town looked, and I thought, well, I thought it would be a good place to..."

She swallowed hard. "You see, I'm married. My husband was in Afghanistan, one of the last to leave Kabul.

"We emailed and Skyped whenever we could, and he seemed fine, just talked about the weather and the food, mostly.

"But at the end, he seemed different. He wasn't sleeping well, and kept looking over his shoulder when we were Skyping. His emails became mostly just swearing and complaining..."

The tears finally breeched her lower lids and they came pouring out.

"He had to leave his interpreter behind and he disappeared, and his family was killed."

Ms. Pat's hand flew to her mouth in horror, her other hand reaching out to touch Tracy's arm. Now her eyes were filled with tears as well.

"I thought Jack might do better living in a small town. In the city, all the noises shatter his nerves. He punches things –"

Ms. Pat now squeezed Tracy's arm.

"No, no, not me. He punches pillows, the couch cushions. He has horrible nightmares. He's seeing an online therapist through the VA but it doesn't seem to be helping."

She stopped to wipe her eyes. Ms. Pat handed her a clean dishtowel and Tracy hid her face in it for a moment, catching her breath. She lowered it and looked at Ms. Pat, seeming a bit ashamed for unloading on her.

"Tracy, you are so brave. I'm so glad you told me this. I knew something was up, but didn't know what. Why don't you just wait here a minute, I'll be right back."

Tracy nodded and took some even breaths, composing herself. It hadn't been as hard as she thought it would be to talk to Ms. Pat after all.

Ms. Pat went back out to the diner and made her way to Olivia's table.

"Hello, Olivia, Liam. Olivia, are you and Emma still looking for a cook and household help at the inn? If so, I think I have just the person."

—⚶—

Tracy spoke with Olivia, then went back to the inn with her and Liam to meet with Emma. When Emma heard Tracy had Ms. Pat's recommendation, she didn't hesitate, and hired her to start as soon as she was able. Tracy and Jack could even have the small guest room in the attic. It couldn't be used anyway, needing more renovations than any other section of the house. Tracy would train with Olivia and Emma, then the Turner sisters would be freed from most of the cooking and cleaning.

The next weekend, Tracy and Jack Nelson arrived with what Emma thought was a very small amount of luggage. She hoped Tracy wouldn't leave them in the lurch with an inn full of guests during the busy season, but she had prayed for help, and here was help. She would not question how the Lord provided as it says in Philippians 4:19, *"And my God will supply every need of yours according to his riches in glory in Christ Jesus."*

"Why don't you two get settled, then come downstairs and we'll take a tour," Emma suggested. "We've got some nice garden paths and a lot of renovations going on."

"Yes, we're working on the gardens now too. You'll be able to see the livestream now that we have good internet," Olivia added cheerfully.

Jack managed a thank-you and Tracy smiled slightly. They made their way up the stairs.

"Olivia, do you think this was a good idea?" Emma asked, her eyes trailing after Tracy and Jack.

"Sure, it'll be fine. It was Ms. Pat's idea. She wouldn't have suggested it if there was anything majorly wrong. Maybe they're just shy."

Emma nodded thoughtfully.

"And besides," Olivia added, "no more 'time to make the donuts!' Yes!" She held her hand out for a fist bump. Emma would have preferred a high five, but bumped her little sister's knuckles and chuckled.

Jack and Tracy came downstairs. Emma noticed Jack was wearing army boots and carried a beige boonie hat. Yes, he looked about the age to be an Afghanistan veteran. Things were starting to make sense.

The four of them went out through the kitchen and started walking on one of the paths. They came across Liam, who was still working on the compost bins. He stood up and smiled as the group approached.

"Hey," he said in greeting.

"Hey," replied Jack. It was the first time anyone had heard him speak.

"Liam, this is Jack, Tracy's husband."

Liam held out a hand and Jack shook it. "Glad to meet you. Taking the tour?"

Jack nodded.

"We'll be widening these garden paths next and building some raised beds for the garden, make it wheelchair accessible. You handy with tools?"

Jack nodded.

"Great, maybe you can help. We've already got some seedlings started in the plastic-covered greenhouse. Olivia figures to have people come in for cooking classes using the fresh herbs and stuff."

Jack nodded again. Tracy smiled.

"Okay, so, let's keep walking. Our other guest uses the old garden shed as an artist's studio. He's been... well... we've been..." Emma was a bit flustered. She'd never really articulated her new relationship with Daniel to anyone outside the family.

Olivia simply said, "They're dating."

Emma blushed.

Jack nodded.

Tracy smiled.

Liam chuckled.

Jack smiled.

Jack smiled!

That night at dinner, Reverend Sam felt truly blessed. He had his two daughters with him, two young men who were paying guests – and one was dating his eldest daughter – and two new faces, the cook/housekeeper and her veteran husband. At one interaction with Jack, the reverend could spot the PTSD a mile away and trusted that God had put this young man here for a reason. Hopefully, to heal.

After dinner, they made their way to the porch. The weather had truly turned spring-like, and only light jackets and sweaters were needed. There were even tree-peeper frogs singing away in the dark and the deeper sounds of bullfrogs in the distance. Lightning bugs sparkled in the air, making the atmosphere around them quite mystical.

Emma and Daniel took the porch swing, with Jack and Tracy on the bench and the others in chairs. The conversation was pleasant, with Olivia bringing everyone up to speed on her marketing efforts. She was getting more and more inquiries, but still no major reservations, but she was not concerned. She knew God would supply the guests, just as He had their new employees and their wonderful (except for a certain dramatic lady) two guests so far.

The reverend asked Emma how the renovations were going. "Pretty well. A little behind schedule and over budget, but I expected that. Still, if we do get this gardening and cooking thing going, we'll need at least six rooms ready by the first harvest. When will that be?" she asked.

"I expect around ninety days for enough to make some dishes with peas, spinach, and lettuce. The herbs won't be ready for another couple of months after that," Liam replied.

"That's good to know," Emma responded. "I'll check with Harvey to see if he thinks he'll be done by then."

"So how is your sketching going, Daniel?" the reverend asked. "We don't see much of you during the day. Are you going to do a showing here in town for us?"

"The sketching's going well. I actually did a bunch of charcoals, now I'm thinking of bringing out my oils, now that I'll be staying longer." He looked at Emma, wanting to take her hand but thinking that might be a bit too obvious. They just smiled at each other.

"And how are you two liking it here so far?" the reverend asked Jack and Tracy. Tracy barely glanced at Jack and then answered for them. "We like it. It sure beats the city, with all that noise."

"Do the renovations bother you? They're a noisy bunch when they're hammering and sawing."

"No, sir, no bother," Jack said, his mouth a straight line. Tracy didn't say anything, just held his hand.

Daniel took that as a cue and discreetly took Emma's hand as well.

That caught Emma by surprise and she fought the urge to snatch her hand away. Where did that urge come from? She liked Daniel, and there was nothing wrong with holding hands, even in front of her dad. She essentially had his blessing to date Daniel.

Emma realized it was leftover emotional turmoil from dating Byron. When he held her hand it wasn't because he cared about her, it was to show possession, ownership. She had to tell herself, *This is different. Daniel isn't using me for his own social gain. He isn't Byron.*

Her palm became sweaty and her heart rate increased. Daniel could sense her tenseness and wasn't sure if he should let go of her hand. Maybe she was embarrassed? Maybe she'd changed her mind about him? No, she would have said something.

The dilemma was resolved when his cell phone chimed that he had received a text. He released Emma's hand to retrieve it and check the message. His expression became stern as he looked up to the group's expectant faces.

"I have to go into the city. Excuse me." He stood up and made his way inside.

—◆—

Everyone on the porch just looked at each other in surprise. The reverend gestured to Emma with his head to go inside and find out what was going on. She rose and followed Daniel up the stairs.

When she got to his doorway, he was already retrieving his overnight back and some clothes.

"What's going on?" Emma asked. "Is everything all right?"

"Not really," he replied. "Izzy says to meet her at her lawyer's first thing in the morning. She says my contract with her is binding and I have to put on an art show or pay some fine or forfeit my artwork or something, I don't know..." he trailed off, looking around his room for what else he should pack.

"What? Can she do that?" Emma asked more sharply than she'd planned.

"Apparently, yes, she can do that," he snapped.

Emma took a small step backward.

"I'm sorry, Emma, I'm not mad at you. I'm just...mad. I thought this was all behind me, behind us, but here she is, still pulling the strings."

"How long will you be gone?" Emma asked, trying to recover her voice after the prior response from Daniel, again telling herself that he was not Byron, and meant no ill will. The length of time he'd be gone would be a tell. Overnight, and it was no big deal. A few weeks might indicate he would be forced to go back into business with her... or more. Emma had to block her thoughts there to not overreact in this moment, and try to be understanding, knowing how tumultuous the whole situation was with Daniel and Izzy.

"I'll know more tomorrow after the lawyer meeting." He stopped packing and looked at her. "Whatever happens, let's try to stay calm, okay?"

"Sure, yeah, okay. Stay calm. You're going to see your old girlfriend tomorrow, and she has some power over you with this contract, but yeah, let's stay calm." Her attempt to not sound sarcastic, needy, and a bit angry all at the same time was failing very badly.

"You know I don't like this, right?" he said, his own resolve to stay calm going out the window. "We just had a nice dinner and conversation on the porch and then wham, I'm blindsided by this... this... command performance. I don't like it any more than you do."

"I know that. It's just..."

"Just what?"

"Just that, well, you're going to see your ex and it scares me."

Daniel finally stopped to look at Emma, realizing the almost pained look she wore and immediately crossed the room toward her and took her gently in his arms, looking into her face. "Emma, honey, I'm not going to risk what we're building here. And I don't mean the renovations. I mean us, our relationship. I know a good thing when I see one." He smiled, and she smiled back, letting out a long breath she did not even realize she had been holding.

"I'm glad. Okay, let's just take it one day at a time and have some faith that things will work out."

"That's a great attitude. I'll text you when I get there, okay?"

"Okay. Drive safe." She wanted to say I'll miss you, but was already feeling a little ridiculous about her reaction.

"Don't worry. I'll let you know what's going on every step of the way."

As they stood there in each other's arms, the fear each felt for different reasons – Daniel because there could very well be unforeseen repercussions from the business contract, Emma because she might lose Daniel to Izzy – caused them both to cling a little tighter.

When they released their hug, Daniel took Emma's face in his hands and leaned in, gently brushing his lips against hers. Emma put her arms around Daniel's shoulders and reached up to him, kissing him cautiously. He kissed her back, and they stayed that way for a moment.

When they drew back, Daniel was smiling that goofy smile he'd had on his face when he first brought her the flowers and asked her out on a date. That caused her to laugh, and the tension was broken.

"Okay then, text me when you get there. I'll miss you."

"I'll miss you too. Keep the faith." He sealed it with another kiss, grabbed his bag, and walked down the stairs.

—∞—

"What do you mean, minor setback?" Emma nearly shouted. She stopped to count to ten in her head to calm down but only made it to five. "We need to have the rooms ready within ninety days. We've got marketing plans going and Olivia's expecting guests to start arriving within that timeframe. You promised!"

"I know, Miss Emma, but some things are out of my control. The plans for the renovations were all approved by the town council except that one item. Now they're saying there needs to be a major upgrade to the sprinkler system to keep it within code. It's one thing that can't be grandfathered."

Emma was dumbfounded. How could this happen? She'd planned and arranged and met with the permit people multiple times. She counted in her head again and made it to ten this time, looking at Harvey nearly wringing his hands standing before her. She instantly felt regret for her reaction and made reparations.

"I know it's not your fault, Harvey. You've been doing a great job. I'll just need to meet with the council again and figure out a way around this. We can't delay and we can't afford it anyway. This inn is safe and they all know it. We were up to code before the renovations. That shouldn't have made such a huge difference."

Harvey relaxed a bit. "You're right there, Miss Emma. And there was no word of warning, just a quick stop by from the fire marshal saying it wasn't to code. He barely even looked around, then took off in his little red pickup truck. It seemed quite odd to be exact."

"Okay, well, I'm going to take a walk so I can think straight. You can keep on with our plans so we can finish on time. I'm sorry Harvey that I lifted my voice at you, I am getting a bit anxious at this point." Harvey nodded and smiled gently, letting Emma know he understood. He was quite invested in this project as well, wanting the inn to return to its former glory, or even better if he was able. He set his hat straight on his head and went back to work. Emma grabbed her sweater and went out the back door.

As she walked along, her mind was still grappling with this latest news. How? Why? She wished Daniel were here. She felt the absence of his presence as she made her way past the old garden shed, now vacant for a week.

He'd kept her in the loop through texts and phone calls. Izzy's lawyer made it clear. Daniel had agreed to four art shows per year or he'd have to pay Izzy what she would have made from the shows. Daniel now had to hire his own lawyer to try to sort it out.

When she arrived back at the house, she saw Liam working on the raised bed gardens. Some were a foot high on the ground, and some were in boxes at wheelchair height.

He looked up and smiled, then saw the crestfallen expression on her face. He stood up to face her. "What's wrong?"

"The fire marshal says the inn is no longer up to code and we have to put in a huge new sprinkler system or we can't get an occupancy permit. Harvey says we'd essentially have to rebuild the whole inn, because the rafters aren't strong enough to hold the massive pipes. I just don't understand how this could happen."

Liam thought a minute. "But the town approved the plans before the renovations were started, yeah?"

"Yes. I'm not sure what happened, why they changed their minds."

He thought about his sister Avery and her anger that her development project was bumped for the Turner Inn renovations. "Yeah, that is weird." He put down his hammer. "I'm just going to go into town for something, be right back."

Emma was even more befuddled at his response, but nodded and watched as he quickly hopped on one of the mopeds and buzzed off toward town.

—◇—

"What makes you think I had anything to do with it?" Avery questioned defensively.

"Because, sis, you're mad that her project was approved just before you tried to get yours done. I'll ask you straight. Did you sabotage the inn's upgrades by going to the fire marshal to complain?"

"I didn't sabotage anything. I simply went to dinner with a man who happens to be the fire marshal and may have mentioned that the inn is very old and I was afraid it might burn down."

Liam sighed in exasperation. "What is it with you? Why would you do that? You must have known he'd react the way he did."

"No, I didn't. And besides, the inn *is* very old –"

Liam held up a hand. "Don't. Just do the right thing and fix this mess you made."

He turned around, hopped on the moped, and sped back to the inn.

"Well! Bossy little thing, isn't he," she said to herself. Liam didn't butt into her business very often so when he did, she knew it was important to him. He was the only family she had left and he really was important to her. She couldn't risk losing her brother. He had planted the seed of conviction in her all right, and she did feel a bit guilty now faced with what she had done.

Avery was torn. It seemed she'd spent most of her life competing with Emma. Was it time to hang up the gloves?

She knew the fire marshal would be having lunch at the diner. She sighed, put on fresh lipstick, and went to fix the mess she'd made.

CHAPTER 12

TURNING POINTS

*N*ow *I know why people say long-distance relationships don't work,* thought Emma as she logged onto Skype again. This was her nightly time with Daniel to keep in touch while he was in the city letting the lawyers work things out with his contractual obligations.

Her computer was ringing and she answered, seeing Daniel's face on her screen. He didn't look happy.

"Hi," Emma said. "Any news?"

"Yes, and it's all bad," Daniel replied. "My lawyer doesn't see a way out of this contract."

"What does this mean?" Emma asked. "How much longer will you have to stay in the city?" She didn't like sounding so needy. She was very close to whining. She cleared her throat and sat up straighter in her chair, shaking her head as if to shake away the unhappiness.

Daniel sighed. "The contract was for four years, and I've only served one year of it."

Served. An interesting word choice. Like a prison sentence.

"So, you're saying you have to stay there for three more years? I don't understand how this could happen."

Daniel looked dejected. "I'll tell you how it happened. But you're not going to like it. And it's pretty embarrassing, in hindsight."

Emma waited, trying not to tap her fingers on the desktop impatiently.

"Well, when I first came to the city, I didn't have any kind of following. I had no name in the art world, not even an online presence. Looking back, I can't believe I even took the risk. I just up and moved, like some kid thinking I'd be discovered or somehow get a big break or become instantly famous or something, I don't know,"

"I was finally allowed by one of the restaurants to sketch their customers' portraits while they were dining at the outdoor café area. I'd ask permission, make the sketch, then offer it to the patron. I wasn't allowed to ask for money, so I just relied on their generosity."

Emma was trying to envision this scenario. Daniel was a quiet introvert. It must have been very difficult for him to approach perfect strangers.

Daniel continued. "I actually got pretty good at it. I sort of pretended I was in some street side café in Paris. I even started wearing a beret. I'd just sort of sit back and sketch until a couple noticed me, then I'd say something like, I'd love to sketch you, would you mind? Most of the time they said sure, go ahead. Then I'd turn the board around and show them. Usually, the lady would be pleased and would gesture to the guy to give me some money. Sometimes, I had to look hungry – sometimes I *was* hungry – and hint that it might be worth something someday, then they'd hand over some money."

"But why did you even go there in the first place? Why not just stay home and try to build a following?" Emma asked.

Daniel looked even more uncomfortable than before. "Emma, we've not known each other for very long. We don't know all that much about each other. I've learned a lot about you from sitting on the porch with you and your family after dinner. But we've never really gone into my past."

Emma thought about it. "That's true, but I figured you're a very private person, and if there was anything I really needed to know, you would tell me. The you I've come to know these past few months seems okay. You told us about Izzy, and my father thought it was okay for us to start dating –"

"Did I hear my name?" Izzy inquired, sauntering up to the screen. She leaned down next to Daniel to get her face in the camera. Daniel tried to stretch away but she clutched his arm like a hawk strangling a mouse.

"Emma, is that you?" Izzy nearly purred. "How lovely to see you. Daniel and I were just heading out to meet and greet some art gallery owners so he'll have to cut this short. You understand, I'm sure."

Emma was speechless. What was *she* doing in Daniel's apartment?

Daniel looked like he wanted to crawl under the rug. If Emma hadn't been so confused and taken aback – and yes, jealous – she might have felt sorry for him.

"Daniel?" was all Emma could manage.

"I'm sorry, Emma. I'm obligated to do this thing. The sooner I can get those four art shows in for this year, the sooner I can get out of here." He looked hard at Izzy. Izzy seemed a bit surprised and backed away a bit, as if she'd been stung. She finally stood up.

"Well there's gratitude for you. I pick you up as a sidewalk caricaturist and turn you into a sought-after artist, and that's the thanks I get? You're lucky the contract was only for four years." She turned on her heel and stormed out, calling over her shoulder. "Hang up and let's get going."

"Emma, honey, please say you understand. I'm stuck here for now, but it won't be forever. I can make my art anywhere, so as soon as these shows are scheduled I can come back to Graceville. To you." He looked at her pleadingly.

Emma spoke slowly. "I wish I could say I understand, Daniel. My mind is going to some pretty dark places right now though –"

"Please believe me, I really don't want to be here. I want to be with you. I want to be sitting on the porch swing, listening to your dad tell stories and your sister and Liam laughing. I want to hold your hand and reassure you that I... I... I miss you terribly, and I can't wait to get back."

Daniel slowly put his hand up to the screen.

Emma did believe him. She hadn't seen through Byron until the very end of their relationship, and she was afraid she might be missing some signals here that Daniel was just as much a cad as Byron was.

Then she was afraid she was looking too hard for similarities between Byron and Daniel. If she spent her whole life on edge, watching out for narcissistic tendencies in everyone she met, her life would be miserable and frightening.

With all the turmoil in her mind and heart, she couldn't speak. She just brought her hand up to the screen and placed her fingertips against Daniel's.

His face softened. He nodded.

She nodded too and with her free hand, ended the video call. Emma still could not hold back the single tear that tipped over the edge of her left eye. She quickly wiped it away and rose from her chair. She had work to do.

—⁕—

The guest room and common area renovations had been completed. All that was left in those areas was to refurbish the linens and wall hangings.

Tracy had done a remarkable job taking on the cooking and had polished everything to a shine. Jack helped Liam out in the gardens and they were looking great, with widened pea stone pathways and raised beds filled with a light, fluffy soil mixture and a variety of seedlings and plants. There was greenery was everywhere. You could tell this was a place of life.

The garden shed Daniel had been using as an art studio sat vacant. No one went inside, and everyone had long since stopped asking Emma when he'd be returning, as it obviously upset her too much. She retreated quickly when someone brought up his name or anything pertaining to her knowledge of his whereabouts.

Unbeknownst to anyone, Daniel had kept in touch with the reverend, just to let him know he wasn't playing around with Emma's heart and that he truly wanted to do the right thing. He sought wisdom from the reverend, who in turn shepherded this young man as best he could without interfering in his daughter's relationship with him. It was a tricky road to navigate, but with prayer and the guidance he received in return, he thought he was headed down the right path- but he knew also that he had to fulfill his contracts with Izzy or face the consequences.

Olivia continued researching the inn's and the town's history, looking for content to add to the inn's website and social media feeds. Miss Evelyn at the library was a great help here. She seemed to know what Olivia wanted even before asking as she dove deeper into the inn's past. Even with the internet signal strong at the inn, Olivia enjoyed hopping on a moped and heading to the library to listen to the librarian's stories of the past. It seemed she knew so much of the history that just reading would not provide. The feelings of the community at certain times in history and what truly was going on in their very small, remote part of the world.

That night on the porch after dinner, Olivia asked, "Emma, when do you think we can start allowing guests in? I'm getting more and more inquiries every day but I've been putting them off until we get the occupancy permit."

"Funny you should ask," Emma replied. "I heard from the fire marshal today. He said he's ready to come back out and do a 'more thorough' inspection." She made air quotes around *more thorough*. She had to admit it was a surprise to get a return phone call from him.

"Is that a good thing?" Olivia asked.

"Normally, I wouldn't think so. It's like having the IRS tell you they want to do a more thorough audit of your tax return. But his tone was light, almost happy."

"I'm sure it's a good thing," Liam interjected. "I'd say we can start accepting reservations real soon."

"Is there enough from the gardens for your dinner-guests-doing-the-cooking plan?" the reverend asked. "I haven't been out there in a while, been a bit busy with church business. I apologize, I see you guys doing so much here that it has inspired me to do more with the community."

"In a couple more weeks we'll have peas, lettuce, radishes, and spinach. So we could make salads and omelets, at least. Maybe even some cherry tomatoes."

Olivia looked odd for a moment then spoke, "I guess we need some chickens too, huh?"

Everyone just burst out laughing.

Emma looked at Liam appreciatively. This young man had come into their lives and improved things in so many ways. He started as a paying guest, then started with the hardscaping and gardens, now with his positive attitude about the fire marshal approving the sprinkler system so they could get the occupancy permit, she just really valued his presence. Emma also noticed the attention he paid to her sister and realized: as hard as it was to admit that he probably wouldn't be helping as he had if she didn't have such a wonderful sister. She knew he had a great heart but she also saw the looks when he thought no one was looking. She did not know whether her sister realized this man had a humongous crush on her or not. Probably not. Her sister was a force to be reckoned with and was mostly blind to anything romantic.

Tracy reached out and squeezed Jack's hand. "And you helped with all that," she said proudly. He just nodded, going back to the faraway look he had so often.

"You've all done very well," said Reverend Sam. "I feel truly blessed to have all of you here. I never in a million years thought my family would need to come to my rescue but here you are. You've turned things around beautifully, Emma. And Olivia, I don't know how to express how proud of you I am as you do you with all this technical and online stuff and your internet thing. You both are truly amazing, and I thank you for coming to the aid of an ol' dad."

Olivia was pleased he was proud of her, but wished he'd stop calling it an *internet thing*.

"And you young people are just what this place needed," he addressed Tracy, Jack, and Liam. "I'm very grateful to you all. My prayers are being answered one by one. My great-grandfather would be so pleased."

"Oh, that reminds me, Dad," Olivia said. "I've been doing more research at the library and found out a few more things about your great-grandparents. Some folks in town blamed your great-grandfather's wife for bringing the 1918 flu epidemic to Graceville."

"What?" the reverend blurted, totally taken off-guard.

"Wait, Dad, there's more." Olivia did not notice her dad's reaction and continued on vehemently with her finding as if it was the next piece of the absurd puzzle of the letters, "I found out from newspaper clippings that a traveling carnival show had come through just two weeks before the first Mrs. Turner arrived. As you know, it usually takes two weeks for the flu to incubate before the symptoms appear."

"The *first* Mrs. Turner?" the reverend asked, mouth agape.

"Yes, Dad. She died of the flu shortly after she married your great-grandfather. There wouldn't have been time to have a baby. So I figured I'd go through the marriage register and sure enough, in 1919, your great-grandfather remarried, and a year after *that* was when your grandfather was born."

Olivia sat back in her porch chair, victorious.

"Wait, how did you know to even look into this?" Emma asked.

"Daniel is always talking to Ms. Evelyn at the library and she said the first Mrs. Turner, brought the flu to town. I guess the descendants of the people who died are still upset, not knowing the full story."

The reverend needed a moment. He was unaware of any of these facts and also of the fact that there were still feelings regarding such an issue in the community that he served as leader of their church.

"Well that is a pickle," the reverend said after trying to recover quickly from the shock of these newly found facts. "How are we going to set the record straight?"

"We could erect a plaque," said Jack.

All eyes turned to him in surprise. Jack never spoke, just sat there, usually gazing out into the atmosphere, appearing stand-offish, so everyone gave him his space. No one even realized he was listening to their conversation because it was apparent that he was clearly uninterested.

"A plaque?" inquired the reverend gently.

"Sure, a plaque to the fallen of the flu epidemic. Brought to town by a traveling carnival, like Olivia said. Once it's in writing, it'll outweigh the gossip. Put it in brass, make it look official."

Everyone was silent for a moment as they just simply stared at Jack. After a moment, Jack started to move restlessly, as if to leave. Then everyone nodded thoughtfully. Then everyone smiled.

"Great idea, dude," Liam said with a smile, and then even more excitedly, "We can get working on it tomorrow."

"Wow, what an awesome idea." said Olivia with renewed enthusiasm and thoughts of new marketing ideas in her eyes.

Tracy's eyes beamed and filled with tears and she squeezed her husband's hand with all her might, hoping he knew how proud she was.

Emma was just tired, trying to show how happy and grateful for her family and friends she was, but feeling a sense of loss........of Daniel. Just being there.

—⚬⚬⚬—

Emma was bracing herself for her Skype session with Daniel. The last one had gone so badly, she'd felt a dark cloud over her the whole next day.

As the Skype chimes sounded, she took in a breath and said a little prayer. "Lord God, please help us navigate through this season. Please show us and guide in all our ways. Please help us to know the right paths to take and that if we're meant to be together, please make our ways known. If not Lord, please let us know as painlessly as possible and again show us that your ways are greater than ours. Amen."

Daniel connected just as she was finishing. "Amen?" he asked. "You were praying?"

"Yes," Emma replied. "I was praying for us. It seems like we have a lot going against us, so I was praying for smooth sailing."

Daniel smiled and instantly felt the attraction again with this woman that he had grown to love. "I like that...no, I love that. You're a good woman, Emma, and I'm lucky to have you in my life. You have no idea the impact you and your family have made on my life and I can never tell you how awesome it is to know people pray and that I may be included in those prayers."

This was more like it. But, she just had to ask. And she HATED asking. "Is Izzy there?"

Daniel shook his head. "No, I'm here alone. There's no reason for her to be here tonight. We've booked two of the four showings, but there's no one to meet tonight."

Emma was relieved, and she knew it showed on her face. "I'm glad. I needed you to be honest about your feelings and whereabouts... and to have you all to myself tonight." She blushed at her honesty.

"Well, what's going on with the inn? Are the renovations finished?"

All tensions resided and Emma and Daniel fell into their easy comraderie, as usual.

"They are almost finished. The fire marshal seems to have had a change of heart for some reason. He said he wants to come out again. Liam seems to think it's a 'good sign'-whatever," Emma threw her hands up at this point, "and hopefully we'll get the go-ahead for the occupancy permit so we can start welcoming guests."

"That's great! But, how does Liam know anything about this?"

Emma thought a moment. "You know, I'm not sure. He seemed very confident though. But then, he always seems confident. He's a good friend... to all of us," she added, not sure why.

"Yes," agreed Daniel, albeit a bit jealous, he wanted Emma's attentions on no other males. Then he began to think of connections, stating, "So different from his sister..." Something was niggling at his brain. "You said it was the fire marshal who was causing the headaches?"

"Yes, why?" Emma was becoming unsettled by his tone.

Daniel remembered seeing Avery in the diner on more than one occasion, seated at the same table as the fire marshal. Would she stoop so low as to sabotage the inn's chances of survival by swaying the fire marshal?

Should he tell Emma of these sightings or keep quiet? This was the woman he loved. But of course he should.

It made sense. If she had, and Liam found out about it, he could have convinced her to ask the fire marshal to back off and approve the sprinkler system. That's how Liam was so confident the negative decision would be reversed. Daniel nodded and decided the Lord God had worked his magic once again.

"I think Liam is an even better friend than we think," he said.

Emma looked at him quizzically.

"Well, anyway, it sounds like things are moving forward." *While I'm stuck here fulfilling my obligations....* Daniel sighed silently, wanting to be there more than anything.

"Yes. Oh, and Olivia found out something. She said you said that Ms. Evelyn said…" Emma laughed. "It sounds like that game telegraph they made us play in school to show how gossip can get distorted." Daniel laughed too.

"It's about the flu epidemic of 1918. Apparently some people in town were blaming Dad's great-grandfather's wife. But actually, Olivia found a newspaper clipping of a carnival coming through town two weeks earlier, and it takes the flu two weeks to incubate, so it must have been the carnival that brought the flu to Graceville, not the first Mrs. Turner."

"That's great news!" Daniel exclaimed. "Well, not great news that people died, but that it didn't have anything to do with your family. Is she going to put that on the website?"

"Yes, and even better, Jack and Liam are going to put a plaque in the garden honoring the Graceville residents who died during the 1918 pandemic, noting that it was the carnival that brought it, not us. And guess what, it was Jack's idea to do it. So proud of him, right?"

"I think it's excellent," said Daniel, "so very cool". He truly loved how everything was falling into place for the family he had quickly grown to love.

"So, not to bring up everybody's past… you were starting to tell me something last time about yours that you felt was important."

"Yes, but I don't want to spoil the mood now. All your news has been good, I don't want to be a downer."

"Honesty might not always be happy news, but it's still better than wondering," Emma replied tentatively. "I don't want to force you to say anything you don't want to say, but I think it's better to have things out in the open, don't you?"

"Right...... well, so we were talking about why I came to the city instead of trying to sell art at home."

"Yes."

Some of his conversations with the reverend were coming to mind. "You know how in the Bible, the people in Jesus's hometown didn't recognize him as the Messiah?"

"Yes..." Emma replied with a bit of trepidation in her voice. Was he going to compare himself to the Messiah? *Just what I need, another Byron, are you serious?...*

"Well..." He paused and tried to control his breathing. He was just about to omit a truth and cover it with Scripture. He was immediately convicted by the Holy Spirit and decided to come clean again.

"Well, that's not why I left my hometown for the city."

Emma looked perplexed. What? Was this man serious? Where was this going?

"What happened was, I was in a relationship with a woman and I wanted to end it but didn't know how, so I told her I was leaving for the city to make a name for myself, then..." he trailed off.

"Then?" Emma prompted.

"Then, I'd come back for her."

Emma did not know immediately how to respond or the questions to ask, she just said, "You'd come back for her? And did you?"

Daniel hung his head in shame. "No. I never contacted her again."

"Daniel... Reynolds!" Emma exclaimed, realizing in pure astonishment, she didn't even know his middle name. "You left a girl hanging and just moved away?"

Daniel did not have the words to respond, knowing anything he said would only make the truth sound worse to this beautiful woman he admired so much.

Emma recovered quickly, "And then you left Izzy and moved to Graceville? I'm sensing a pattern here, Daniel, and it's not a pretty picture."

Daniel instantly became defensive. "It's not a pattern. I just... they just... it's complicated."

"It's not complicated, Daniel. When you break up with someone, you say, I'm breaking up with you, not I'll come back for you. Someone who does that is a –" She stopped herself to count to ten before saying something she'd regret. *Thank God for therapy…*

Daniel began to speak again then just stopped as he looked in the small rectangle of the computer and could see the anger in her face. He knew she was right. "Well, what do you expect me to do? Go back there and tell her I'm *not* coming back for her? Don't you think that would be worse? She's probably already moved on."

"No, leaving her hanging is definitely worse. You have no way of knowing if she's moved on or not. That is a despicable thing for ANY human to do to another."

Emma felt herself floundering. She found herself not capable of even counting to one, much less to ten to calm down. She could even not think straight.

Daniel continued on though, as Emma just blinked and listened, "Actually, I could try to find her on Facebook and see her status. Maybe she's married with a couple of kids by now."

Emma didn't miss a beat, "And maybe she's pining after the guy who said he'd come back for her. Daniel, you have to see her and talk to her, and face-to-face, not over email. Only a coward would 'spy' on her now after to determine how she feels. Social media seems to be such a mask for everything these days." She instantly regretted using the words coward and spying, but it was out and there was no getting it back.

Daniel did not speak for what seemed like forever and in that time Emma sensed within herself that she had meant every word of what she said after this elongated moment of silence.

"Fine," he grumbled. "I know you're right but I don't like it. I will go to see her as soon as I can get away from here. I'll make sure she's moved on."

"Good," said Emma. There was nothing else to say at this point.

"Well, I'd better go," said Daniel morosely. "I wish our conversation had gone better. Talk soon." He put his hand up to the monitor.

Emma didn't make eye contact, she didn't want to see his emotions, but she put her hand up to the monitor to match his, and quickly signed off.

—⁂—

The doorbell rang just as Daniel was about to turn in for the evening. He was just tired, emotionally, physically, mentally, every kind of way... and just wanted to be left with his thoughts to sort them out for just a bit.

He looked out the peephole. Izzy.

He stopped a minute to pray for strength. And felt decidedly calmer. *Well, the good reverend's influence, no doubt.*

He opened the door. "Izzy, what do you want?"

"Is that any way to greet someone?" Izzy countered, walking past him into the apartment uninvited. She had worn a very low-cut dress with no bra or underwear and very sexy high heels which she knew accentuated every curve and shape of her body. She used her most sultry voice, "I was in the neighborhood and thought I'd stop by," She realized as she spoke that it sounded unconvincing even to her own ears.

"Seriously, Izzy, what do you want from me?" Daniel asked, almost pleading. He remembered Emma's words. "Why are you here? We are broken up. Broken. Up. No longer a couple. Not in love. Not even in lust. Not business partners – not by choice, anyway. So, what do you want from me?"

Izzy was a bit stunned. "I want you," she blurted, surprising herself. "Yes, I wanted you for the money you could bring in once *I made you famous.*" She just had to add that part. "But, Daniel, I really like being a couple. It's not just the money. I want you."

"Since when? You made it clear when I left for Graceville that you were only in it for the money. What changed?"

"I heard the way you were talking with Emma the other night on Skype, how gentle you speak to her. It's like she's... precious to you, ... and I...well, *I* want to be precious to you."

Daniel looked at Izzy as if he was seeing her for the first time. The powerful businesswoman with all the connections in the art world, the beautiful young woman who could turn any man's head. Those images were gone and in front of him stood a scared child, unsure of what she stood for, who she was, and even why she was there.

Daniel knew Izzy came from a broken home. Her dad had left when she was about seven years old. It had been pretty horrible, with her mother left to raise her in poverty. Suddenly, it all made sense.

"Izzy," he said more gently, but in a brotherly way, "I'm not your dad. I can never fill that place in your heart that he left empty."

Izzy's lip started to quiver and tears started to pool in her eyes. She wanted to lash out but couldn't find the words.

Daniel continued. "But there is someone who can. It's our heavenly Father."

Izzy sniffled. "You surprise me, Daniel, talking about God. I suppose that's Emma's dad's doing, thumping his Bible at you every chance he gets. That whole family acts as if they are holier-than-thou. You've never talked about God before. What's going on? Why don't we just go to bed like we always do?"

Daniel maintained his composure, almost as if it was the Holy Spirit speaking through him. "He doesn't thump his Bible, Izzy, but he does quote from it. And the things he says make sense and... they bring me peace. I think they can bring you peace too."

"I don't need, peace, Daniel, I just need you!" Izzy countered, reaching for him.

Daniel countered her moves easily and gently and said, "No, you can't have me. But you can have a relationship with a Father who will never leave you. Never forsake you. A Father who will never let you down, Izzy," He walked over to the coffee table and picked up his Bible. "Here, I want you to have this."

Izzy scoffed. She had thrown many like it before straight into the garbage. How dare he block her advances and try to offer her a book- a BOOK?

"No, seriously, take it. There is some writing in there in red ink. Those are the words Jesus spoke. Just take a glance at them. Take this home with you and just open it and read those red words, a few pages at a time. You have to move on from me, and this is a safe way to get the love you need. No matter what, Izzy, I do care about your eternal life."

Izzy did not know what moved her to grab the 'useless' book Daniel was offering, but she did, holding it as if were a hand grenade.

"You can even go on Biblegateway.com and have it read to you." He knew one of her weak spots. "If you choose the King James Version of the Bible, the guy narrating has a British accent."

She perked up a bit, realizing how well Daniel knew her likes, but still looked doubtful. She peered back at him, wondering if he was truly serious, but realized his eyes held a look of peace she had never seen before. She was astounded and silent and curious. Being speechless was a new thing for Izzy.

"Just try it. It's helped me face some things about myself I wanted to avoid. Running away from you to Graceville was not one of my better moments. I'm sorry, Izzy. I should have made a clean break of it on the up and up instead of running like a... coward."

Izzy was as surprised by his honesty as she had been about her own. She wiped her nose and held the Good Book a little less gingerly, bringing it to her chest. She needed something and she could never find the comfort or the peace of what she felt she truly needed. No one had ever stood their ground with her so simply and humbly as this man just had. No one had ever refused her. She always got what she wanted, but for some odd reason she felt the need to back down, for once. "Okay, Daniel."

She came to realize she had no other words, so she just smiled weakly and made her way to the door, turning to face him. Her eyes were already shining with tears.

"Thanks," was all she said, and she meant it.

CHAPTER 13

UNEXPECTED ALLIANCES

"Will you look at that?" said Susan Sheffield, Harvey the contractor's wife. She was sitting in the Main Street Diner with some of her coworkers from the school cafeteria. "I don't know what that Avery is up to now, but it's surely nothing good."

The other ladies nodded sagely in agreement. They were no fans of the town council, which kept their school budget so low, the teachers had to pay for school supplies and run bake sales and car washes for sports equipment.

Avery was seated at a table with some members of the town council. If the batting of her eyelashes was any indication, she wanted something big and she wanted it badly. The ladies leaned in as unobtrusively as they could to hear more.

"I know you're very busy, gentlemen. I've tried repeatedly to get on your calendar but had to ambush you here instead!" Avery laughed, leaning forward and putting her hand on the oldest councilman's arm. He chuckled and turned pink. One of the other men chuckled but the third did not. Avery decided to ignore him and focus on the other two.

"Councilman Sneed, your family has been in Graceville for generations. You surely know how this was nothing but forest and pastureland for fifty years before the Second World War."

Councilman Sneed nodded, trying hard not to look at her hand on his arm—or her chest pushing tightly against her suitcoat buttons, making them pucker. *She sure does have great... charisma!* he thought.

This did not go unnoticed by Avery, who straightened her back a bit. The ladies at the next table nearly choked on their coffee at her blatant effort.

"When our brave soldiers came home after four brutal years of battle and bloodshed, they had nowhere to go. The country was overrun and there was a severe housing shortage. You've seen the Jean Arthur movie *The More the Merrier*? Soldiers and other patriots sleeping on cots in hotel lobbies."

The two smitten councilmen nodded; the third, Councilman Brooks, simply sat back to watch the spectacle, wishing she'd just get to her point.

Avery clucked her tongue and shook her head. "It was shameful. But it was developers who saved the day, coming to places like Graceville and clearing land to build homes for our poor, homeless soldiers and their brave and patient families. It surely was the greatest generation." At this, she patriotically put her hand over her heart and bowed her head. Councilman Sneed and the other man bowed their heads also. Councilman Brooks tried hard not to groan but did let out a sigh at this dramatic performance.

Avery looked up and realized she had to move things forward quickly. "Gentlemen, what I am proposing is along those same lines. You know I missed the opportunity to present my development request to the town council by mere days because Emma Turner came home—unexpectedly—and beat me to the punch.

"Just what is her rush?" she asked in an accusing tone. "Why is she in such a hurry to open her doors to strangers? What was she doing in the city these past ten years that made her rush home and start tearing the place apart?" She left the questions hanging in the air, hoping the councilmen would have fertile ground in their minds for the seeds of discord she was planting.

"What I am proposing, gentlemen, is much more aboveboard. A development along the side of the road where there's nothing but a few empty lots and some scrub brush. A place for our townspeople to shop, eat, and gather together in community.

"Picture a one-stop shop store where you could get everything from clothing to pet food to groceries. Perhaps an eatery where you could quickly grab a bite to eat without even getting out of your car. A gymnasium where people could go after work to release tension and get to know their neighbors and coworkers outside of business hours.

"That, gentlemen, would put us on the map and maybe instead of people just driving through, they'd consider spending their money here in

Graceville. Think of the income from travelers and tax revenue from the businesses!" she finished victoriously and sat back in her chair, beaming at finally getting her scheme out in the open.

Councilman Brooks, formerly recalcitrant, now leaned forward, seeing right through her. "You paint a pretty picture, Miss Avery. Please describe this shopping center, eatery, and gymnasium in more detail, if you please."

The smile on Avery's face froze but she tried not to lower her eyes in a sign of untruthfulness. She had every right to build her development; as much right as Emma had to renovate her inn.

"Councilman, you ask a very wise question. We are so lucky to have you as a town leader," she schmoozed. The ladies at the next table nearly guffawed, but had to give her credit for her acting ability.

"I've been in talks with various corporations about opening a facility here in Graceville. The two options that would bring in the most dollars—for Graceville," she quickly added, "are an Amazon distribution center or a Walmart."

Councilman Sneed now looked almost terrified as he involuntarily jerked his arm away from her. "A Walmart? In Graceville? That would never fly," he said, now nearly hyperventilating. "We would be drummed off the council for even considering the notion!"

"And the eatery where we can get food quickly without even getting out of our cars? A McDonald's, am I right?"

Avery's frozen smile now started to twitch at the corners. "Well, yes. What's more American than burgers and fries? And think of the jobs it will create for the young people in town? There's nothing else for them to do but move to the city, which is what I should have done—"

She stopped herself. They didn't need to know how bitter she was that others had gone away and seen a bit of the world while she had stayed home out of fear of leaving.

"Which is what I *would* have done," she corrected, "except I love Graceville so much."

The ladies at the next table nearly applauded her quick thinking.

"And this after-hours gymnasium. What is that, exactly?" asked Councilman Brooks, the other two councilmen now looking at her expectantly, blinders off.

Avery didn't try to sugarcoat this one. "It's called 24 Hour Fitness. It offers workouts, classes, and personal training."

"I've heard of that place," said Councilman Brooks. "They teach boxing there, don't they?"

"Kickboxing, actually," noted the third councilman. "They're a fight club."

At that, Susan Sheffield stood up with a loud scraping of her chair, nearly knocking it over. The other ladies stood up too, ready for battle.

Susan marched around the table and stood tall facing Avery. "Avery Thompson, you've gone too far. We will not allow our young people to be exposed to a fight club. There is enough chaos in the world, and I will not have you bringing it to our doorstep. Graceville is a quiet, peaceful community and I will do everything in my power to stop this scheme of yours!" she said forcefully.

The other ladies shuffled forward, nodding their heads and standing behind Susan. The troops had found their leader.

"And as for you," Susan now turned to the councilmen, who stood in a quaint show of respect for a lady coming to their table. Susan softened. "You've kept our budget so low for so long in an effort to 'control spending.'" She made air quotes. "How could you, in all good conscience, even consider this horrible idea?" She made eye contact with each in turn and to their credit, they did not lower their eyes but met her gaze with honest contrition.

"Speaking for myself," said Councilman Brooks, "I will not consider this idea. It's bad for Graceville, plain and simple."

"Nor will I," added Councilman Sneed. The third looked at Avery almost apologetically but shook his head no.

Susan and the ladies nodded. "Good," she stated more calmly. "We'll discuss the school budget later. For now," she looked at Avery, "this discussion is closed." She turned on her heel, marched up to the counter where she paid Ms. Pat, who had been watching the entire show, and the battalion of school workers walked out, heads held high.

Avery remained seated, stunned at the turn of events. Smile gone and tears threatening, she cleared her throat, knees too weak to even stand.

"Avery, you've got on the wrong side of the school ladies and there's not much chance of mending that fence as far as I can tell," said Councilman

Brooks gently. "You tried to pull one over on us. You let slip a little while ago that you wished you had left Graceville after high school like other young folks did."

Avery looked up at him, too numb to speak.

"Maybe now would be a good time for you to do just that."

The councilmen quietly pushed in their chairs and made their way to the counter, leaving the money for their lunches with Ms. Pat and walking out.

—m—

When word got out about Avery's development scheme and trying to throw shade on Emma's plans to renovate the Turner Inn, the townsfolk rallied around Emma and her family. All of a sudden, everyone wanted to lend a helping hand or a word of encouragement

As Olivia rode her moped to the library, she noticed quite a few people waving and smiling at her. She didn't want to let go of the handlebars to wave back, so just nodded and smiled. *Curious.* Graceville was a friendly place, but not usually this friendly.

"Good morning," said someone walking past the library as Olivia was parking her moped.

"Good morning," she responded.

"Fine day today, Miss Turner," said another passerby.

"Yes, it is," Olivia replied, a little suspiciously. She walked up the steps to the library with a few patrons leaving the building and greeting her with good mornings.

"How are renovations going at the inn?" asked a man who held the door open for her with a flourish.

"Good, thanks." *Okay, that was just weird.*

"Good morning, Olivia. I haven't seen you in a while," greeted Evelyn Miller as Olivia entered the library. "Your internet connection at home must be fulfilling your needs."

Olivia greeted the friendly librarian with a smile. "Yes, Ms. Miller, I've spent many hours online building our website and following Emma's marketing plan. There are still some historical things I need to learn about our inn and Graceville to beef up our content."

Miss Miller smiled. "Well, if you're asking 'where's the beef?' it's here!" she laughed, mimicking the elderly lady in the old Wendy's TV commercial.

Too young to remember those commercials, Olivia nodded politely, not sure what she thought was so funny. Miss Evelyn smiled and shook her head.

"Never mind, dear. How can I help you?"

"I was wondering if I could take pictures of some of the library's old photos to put up on my website. Do you know if they're copyrighted or anything?"

"I don't believe so. Some are signed by the photographer, but most of them have no attribution. You might want to check with an attorney, but as far as I'm concerned, as long as you don't use a flash, there should be no problem."

Olivia nodded. Just like in a museum, some artwork could be harmed by the flash.

"Thanks." She hesitated. "Also, not to sound paranoid or anything, but is today a holiday or something? All the way here people were being, well, really nice. Even more so than usual," she added so as to not sound paranoid.

"I expect they're just happy you're here and wish you well on your inn renovations."

"I guess..." Olivia replied doubtfully. "Just seems a little weird."

"Well, there's weird and then there's weird," was all the librarian would say.

Olivia, baffled, pulled out her cell phone and made her way to the history section of the library.

CHAPTER 14

GRACE REVEALED

The Turner Inn was bustling with activity in preparation for their grand reopening on the Fourth of July. Almost all the renovations had been finished. Harvey Sheffield was just working on the attic loft Tracy and Jack had been using as their apartment.

Daniel had returned after finishing his four annual showings in just two months, fulfilling his contractual agreement with Izzy. She had tried her best to thwart him and make him stay, but in truth, her efforts waned after she started reading the Bible he'd given her.

It really was fascinating. She didn't understand a lot of it, but wanting to be a step ahead of things, she had gone to the end of the book to find out what happens next, just like any book she read. She understood there would be a huge battle and lots of calamity and suffering, but that the good guys would win in the end.

Always wanting to be on the winning end of things, Izzy had searched online for an explanation, a translation of what the book of Revelation really meant. After coming across websites and YouTube channels about end times and prepping, she wisely decided to find a Bible study group with real people so she could judge for herself whether they were just trying to scam her or really knew what they were talking about.

She enjoyed meeting weekly with these women. Some were like her, just beginning to look for answers in the Bible, while others seemed to speak a whole different language. "Christianese" was the term some of them jokingly used when one of the ladies would go off on a tangent.

Daniel was pleased, but still doubtful of Izzy's transformation. She hadn't talked about being born-again or even brought up anything about religion. But when he said he was leaving for Graceville, she hadn't stopped him. No conniving, no power play to keep him in the city. No drama at all.

When he returned to the inn, he was a bit disappointed. "Anyone home?!" Daniel called out as he walked in the front door. Silence. He made his way upstairs to his room, noting the updated surroundings and polished woodwork inside and the fresh paint and hanging planters outside. The place looked really good. He was a little ashamed he'd been away during what must have been a very trying time for Emma.

He entered his room and was impressed with the updates. The quilt Emma's grandmother had made was now hanging on a quilt rack and a new comforter set adorned the fluffy bed. The curtains matched the linens, and the walls and ceilings had fresh coats of paint. He went into his en suite bedroom and the porcelain sink and tub were the same but with new faucet hardware and lighting fixtures. It all looked great.

After putting his things away, he made his way downstairs. He was just about to make his way to the kitchen in search of Emma when she appeared at the end of the hallway.

"Hi!" he called out, walking toward her, arms outstretched.

"Hi," she replied, making her way toward him. He noticed she wasn't smiling.

He embraced her and gave her a big squeeze but it was awkward; she didn't really hug him back.

"I missed you," he said, stepping back to look into her eyes. She met his gaze and gave a half-hearted smile.

"Welcome back," she replied, stepping away a little.

"What's up?" Daniel inquired. "Did I catch you at a bad time?"

"No, no, I was just making the rounds, checking on everything before our open house on Saturday."

"Is there anything I can do to help?" Daniel asked, holding both her hands.

"I don't think so," Emma replied, her hands limp in his.

Daniel was silent for a moment, thinking of what to say. He went with the truth. "You don't seem very happy to see me," he finally said. "Has something changed?" He'd been gone for a couple of months but they'd Skyped fairly often. He thought that was enough to hold Emma's interest but maybe he was wrong.

"No, nothing's changed. I'm just preoccupied with the opening." Emma thought that would work, but she felt convicted to tell Daniel the truth. *And when the Holy Spirit convicts you, there's nothing to do but go with it,* she thought.

"Okay, I know you had to stay in the city because Izzy had you trapped in that contract. It's silly, I know, but I feel jealous. And a bit..." She struggled to find the words.

"A bit what?" Daniel asked, eyebrows draw close in anticipation of her next words.

"A bit...I don't know. Let down? Left behind? I feel silly. It's *my* family's inn, and you're a guest here. It's not your responsibility to hold my hand through the renovation process. But it was really difficult. It's almost over now and I guess I feel like a solo rather than a couple."

Daniel was rattled, but tried to remain calm. "I can understand how you would feel that way, and I want you to know how truly sorry I am that my past mess got dragged into our current relationship. There's nothing that can be done about it now, but how about we move forward? Together."

Emma looked doubtful. She'd had reservations from the start. She was still recovering from Byron's emotional and mental abuse, she was a proprietor encouraging a relationship with a guest at her inn. It all just seemed a bit overwhelming. She started to back away.

Daniel held out his hands and gently caught hers, stopping her backward movement. He looked at her earnestly. "Please don't go." He had an idea. "Emma, will you pray with me?"

Emma was caught off guard by his request. "When did you become spiritual?" she asked, honestly curious.

Daniel smiled. At least she was talking. "It's your father's good influence. While I was away, he and I were Skyping too. He gave me some good advice, and did a good job changing his roles between pastor and my girlfriend's father." He gently squeezed her hands.

Emma loved those hands; she had from the first moment she saw them when he was checking in. They were so expressive, so smooth. She looked at them now, holding her hands comfortably. This man was no Byron. He was a good man. A godly man.

She looked up at him with tears in her eyes.

Daniel became concerned. "Honey, why are you crying?"

"I'm so grateful, Daniel. I'd be thrilled to pray with you."

Daniel let out a breath of relief and bowed his head. Emma bowed hers as well.

"Heavenly Father, we love you so much. We are so thankful for all you've given us. This wonderful inn, a loving family, and now we're together at last.

"Lord, please continue to build our faith in you and strengthen us as we proceed through this courtship. Please let me seek and heed wise counsel when it comes to being Christlike and a good man. A godly man."

Emma gasped that he had used the same words she had been thinking. She felt the Holy Spirit moving in their lives.

Daniel looked up a bit. "Is there anything you'd like to add?"

Emma nodded. "Yes. Dear Lord, thank you for all the blessings you've given us, and thank you for bringing us through our dark valleys. There may be more to come but right now, I thank you so very much for this place, my family, and this man you've brought into my life. Please let us know you better and grow in our love for you, and protect us always. In Jesus's name we pray, amen."

"Amen," echoed Daniel.

They looked up and Daniel took Emma in his arms. "Thank you, sweetheart." He kissed her forehead and pulled back a little.

"Emma, I love you."

Emma pulled back a little more, speechless. She wanted to say it back but the words were caught in her throat. She just shook her head, smiling, and threw her arms around his neck, squeezing him tight for a moment before letting him go and stepping back, a huge smile plastered across her face, which was turning pink.

Daniel understood and just laughed, releasing her and taking her hand. "Let's go for a walk."

—⁂—

People started arriving shortly after the parade had ended. Olivia had put posters around town welcoming the locals to the inn's grand re-opening picnic. She hadn't posted anything about it online, instead mentioning that the inn would start their gardening and cooking weekends the following week. This was a special thank-you to the town for their support during the whole renovation process.

Tracy was in her element, chopping and cutting and preparing food for the tables outside. Emma and Olivia were helping in the kitchen while Jack and Daniel were helping Liam get the grounds ready outside. Tables and chairs were set up, trash barrels put out, and potted plants of red, white, and blue set around the seating areas.

The inn looked stunning, freshly painted white with black shutters and festooned with red-white-and-blue streamers. No balloons, because Olivia said they were bad for wildlife, especially in their area, which might choke on the strings.

Reverend Turner, Miss Dot, Miss Evelyn, Gus, and Ms. Pat were seated on the porch on the newly cushioned chairs and benches. They had tried to help, but the young people said they worked hard enough all week and this was a celebration for them too.

"Well, Sam, looks like your girls turned out just fine. They did a great job getting things rolling again," noted Gus.

"They sure did. Their mother would be so proud," the reverend replied. He looked wistfully over at the eating area as the townsfolk came up with their covered dishes and placed them on the appropriate tables, one for main dishes, one for sides and of course, two for desserts.

Liam came by with a bucket of drinks for them. "Thirsty? It's not too hot today, but we've got bottled water, soda, and iced tea. It's important to stay hydrated."

Miss Miller smiled. "I'll have an iced tea," said the librarian.

"That sounds good, Evelyn," said Miss Dot. "I'll have the same, please."

"And I'll have a soda," Ms. Pat added, standing up and passing the bottles and cans around as Liam handed them up to her.

"Same for me, Pat," said Gus. "Sam?"

"Water for now, maybe I'll switch to soda later," the reverend smiled.

Everyone now sat back and enjoyed their refreshments in the shade of the blue-ceilinged porch as Liam walked around offering drinks to the arriving townspeople.

Liam and Daniel got the grill started while Jack went inside to bring out any heavy platters and more ice. With the grills up to temperature, hamburgers, hot dogs, and parboiled chicken were added.

To some, the smell evoked memories of fun outdoor activities and summertime celebrations. To others…

Jack emerged from the kitchen and headed toward the tables with the huge sheet cake, followed by Tracy, Olivia, and Emma with bowls of various salads. He set it down on the dessert table just as the light breeze shifted, bringing the smoke and smell of cooking flesh around him in a cloud.

Jack froze in his tracks, turning pale. He lost his breath and crouched down, his skin clammy, eyes darting everywhere around him, searching for danger. He turned so his back was to the table, almost backing under it.

The people around him stopped talking and stood still, shocked and not knowing what was happening. They didn't know this young man dressed in Army fatigues and dusty boots, but his actions were alarming.

Tracy had just set down her bowl and turned around and saw Jack crouched on the ground. Her hand flew to her mouth to stifle the cry she let out.

Emma and Olivia saw her and turned, thinking maybe Jack had dropped the platter but when they saw him crouched in his defensive position, they knew this was more serious than cake.

Reverend Turner and Gus reacted swiftly, Sam in his capacity of head of household and pastor, and Gus as a former sergeant in the Marine Corps.

"Private Nelson!" Gus called out cheerfully. "Private Nelson!" he repeated as he got closer. "At ease, soldier. It's good to see you here at this picnic." He held out his hand low and slow to help Jack up.

Jack stood to his feet and looked around, still breathing shallowly. Tracy moved quickly to his side and held his arm. The reverend stood on Jack's other side, at arm's length and in front of Jack's peripheral vision where he could be seen and not mistaken as an enemy combatant. He prayed quietly with his hands in front of him in prayer.

"Sergeant Williams, US Marine Corps," said Gus. "Retired," he added.

Jack saluted. Gus returned the salute and held out his hand for a handshake. Jack took it began looking around, coming back to himself.

"Barbeque bother you?" Gus asked. Jack nodded. "Reminds you of combat?"

Jack nodded again.

"Same for me. War is awful, isn't it?"

"Yes, sir. It sure does."

"Good thing we're home now. Why don't you come up on the porch with me and sit a spell? I'd like to hear your thoughts on some things." Gus gestured with his hand toward the porch where the ladies were seated. Reverend Sam nodded to Tracy, who released Jack's arm as he walked away. She turned to Emma and Olivia behind her and they both gave her a supportive group hug.

Miss Dot, Evelyn, and Ms. Pat saw the two veterans heading their way and looked at each other, nodded, and moved into the house. They'd join the party by going through the kitchen and out the back door.

They knew the boy was in good hands now, as Gus had gone through years of therapy through the VA upon returning from Vietnam.

—∞—

Jack and Gus had a nice talk on the porch and rejoined the party later. Jack had agreed to help Gus out at his gas station working on cars now that the inn's renovations were nearly complete. He would also accompany Gus when he visited the VA once a week, Gus to visit with veterans, Jack to go for sign up counseling for PTSD.

As the townspeople were helping themselves to the food tables and finding places to sit, a car pulled up that hardly anyone recognized. Emma recognized it though, and her heart sank. "Byron. What is *he* doing here?" A mini pickup truck with the county seal on the door pulled up next to him.

Byron and another man stepped out of their cars and made their way over to the food tables. Emma intercepted them. "Byron, what are you doing here?"

"Oh, hello, Emma," Byron responded, feigning surprise at seeing her. "I didn't know you were still here. You haven't responded to any of my texts."

"No, I haven't. There's nothing left to say. And who is this?" she said, trying not to sound rude. She was internally relieved that at least she wasn't fearful of Byron. She was mostly just annoyed.

"This," Byron said with a flourish of his hand, "is the county health inspector. His job is to ensure that food served to the public follows strict guidelines so as to avoid outbreaks of illness – such as food poisoning."

"Food poisoning?!" Emma responded a bit too loudly. Some heads nearby turned. Olivia saw Emma talking with Byron and made her way quickly to her sister's side.

"What's going on?" Olivia asked, not minding sounding rude at all.

"Byron has brought the county health inspector. He wants to make sure no one gets..." She looked around, not wanting to draw attention. "Let's go inside."

"We can start right here," the inspector said. "You've got salads that should be refrigerated sitting out on tables."

"Oh, is that a violation?" Byron asked with false innocence.

"I could temp it, but I'm sure it would be above forty-one degrees. And these platters of meat from the grill," he continued. "They are not on any kind of heat source to keep them above one hundred thirty-five degrees. You're putting all these people at risk." He looked around and smiled at Byron, pulling a small notebook from his pocket and beginning to take notes.

"Byron, why are you doing this?" Emma growled between gritted teeth.

"You should have come back to the city with me, sweetums. I had to actually hire an escort to take your place at that important event. You should have come with me but instead you were here playing innkeeper." His voice turned cold. "I couldn't let that go unpunished, now could I?"

Emma involuntarily took a step back. How could she have not seen him for what he was all that time? No matter, she saw right through him now.

"Byron, your problems run deeper than I can deal with. The only one who can help you now is God. I want this to be our final meeting. I wish you the best, and I forgive you, and let you go."

"You forgive me? That's rich. I don't need your forgiveness –"

"Maybe not, but my forgiveness isn't for you, it's for me. It's so I can close the door on what I thought was a relationship and move on with my life. For good."

The inspector, meanwhile, had frozen with pencil in midair, realizing he'd been played. "You told me there was an uncertified catering business refusing to abide by county instructions on food service, with many violations they just threw in a drawer and ignored. Are you telling me this is just a vendetta against an ex-girlfriend? And on a holiday?"

Byron turned to the inspector, momentarily speechless. He was not used to being called out on his dishonesty, and definitely not in public. Many eyes were on them now, wondering what was going on.

Liam came up with his large bucket of ice and some tinfoil trays. "Hey, welcome, join the party. I'm just here to put ice under all these platters and bowls. Want to give me a hand?"

Olivia jumped right in, setting out the trays while Liam filled them with ice and Olivia set the bowls and platters on the ice. Tracy saw what was happening and came out with cling wrap, covering each dish as it was placed on the ice.

"Well, as they say on TV, nothing to see here," said the inspector, snapping his notebook shut and heading back toward his county vehicle.

Reverend Sam made his way through the tables to Emma's side. "Emma?" he merely asked.

One look at the reverend and Byron beat a hasty retreat, nearly tripping over a chair as he walked backward and finally turned and headed for his car. He got in and drove away, not concerned about Emma or the county inspector, only noting how he was one of the tallest and best-looking people at the party.

—⚶—

As the tables were being cleared of plates and cups and people were thinking of starting to leave, the Turners stood on the path behind the tables.

Reverend Turner looked out over the happy crowd of fellow townspeople and smiled. "Friends and neighbors!" he called, getting everyone's attention. "My family and I want to thank you for attending our open house today. You've brought us much joy, and we thank you for your support.

"My daughters, Emma and Olivia, handled the renovations of the inn and the marketing to bring some fine, new guests to Graceville. And they brought us the internet!"

The crowd applauded, nodding their heads in approval.

"Thank you also to Tracy Nelson, who did most of the cooking for this fine meal we've all shared."

Tracy blushed as the crowd applauded. The reverend motioned her over to join them.

"Before you go, we'd like to take you on a brief walking tour of the gardens. Liam Thompson and Jack Nelson did most of the work out here. And there's something special they'd like you to see."

Liam and Jack joined the group and started heading up one of the newly widened pea stone paths. The townsfolk followed along, happy and full and pleased at the outcome of the inn.

As the crowd came to the highest point on the walking paths, the stopped at a small hill with a white sheet covering something. There were a variety of white flowers coming up all around the hill, with a beautiful dogwood tree to one side.

Liam and Jack stood on either side of the sheet. Liam announced, "We wanted to commemorate those lost to the flu pandemic of 1918. The first Mrs. Turner died of it shortly after arriving to Graceville, along with some other people in town. The flu was apparently brought here by a traveling show that came to town two weeks earlier. So, Jack had the idea to erect a plaque in their memory."

He nodded to Jack, and they lowered the sheet to the ground.

The townspeople moved closer to get a look. There were about ten names listed, including the first Mrs. Turner and some other family names from town.

Miss Evelyn and Ms. Pat looked at each other. A traveling show two weeks earlier? It made sense. They were embarrassed at having believed a rumor and not fact-checking it themselves, even though it was told to them by what they thought were credible sources. Lesson learned. They could let that go now.

The Turners had not brought the deadly influenza pandemic of 1918 to Graceville.

CHAPTER 15

LOVE AND NEW BEGINNINGS

By Christmastime, the inn and the town had settled into a nice routine. Guests were expected at the inn every weekend now. Most businesses offered special discounts to Turner Inn guests in return for being allowed to place business cards in a rack in the front parlor of the inn. There had even been a special graveyard tour put on by the Graceville Historical Society at Halloween.

Reverend Sam was pleased that some of the inn's guests attended church services on Sunday mornings. He made sure they were welcomed but not given special treatment. Miss Dot had fresh coffee in the reception area and was always ready to hand out the weekly bulletins she created.

Olivia seemed a bit bored once the initial push to open the inn was complete. Updating the social media accounts every day took only a few minutes, leaving her at loose ends the rest of the day. She wandered down to the library one morning, not sure what she was looking for.

As Olivia sauntered in, Miss Evelyn could tell something was bothering her. "May I help you?" She offered her usual greeting, but it sounded like she was willing to help with more than just books.

"I don't think so, Miss Miller," Olivia responded. "I'm just... I don't know. Bored, I guess."

"Hmm, yes, I can see how that can happen. The after-effects of so much activity all year and now that things are going smoothly, you're not quite sure how to handle it?"

"Yes, exactly!" Olivia said too loudly, immediately offering a silent apology.

"My dear, that's called serenity," Miss Evelyn chuckled. Olivia's eyes widened and she laughed quietly too.

"You're right. I should take it for what it is, a respite from all the hard work. Still, I feel like I should be doing more. Something... I don't know what."

"Well, how is your magazine writing going?" the librarian asked.

"It's going okay. To be honest, I haven't really found any exciting topics lately. Politics are quiet – for now. Climate's a disaster, wars in foreign places. But all those topics are being blogged to death."

"Blogged? Yes, well, what is it you want to do?"

"I wish I knew," Olivia replied, pulling off her mittens. "I guess I'll just sit in the reading room for a while. Maybe something will come to me."

Miss Evelyn had an idea. "That's a good idea. On your way, would you mind putting these books back? I've already catalogued them. You know where the shelves are, yes?"

Olivia looked at the spines of the books and noted the section and placement for each book. "Yes, ma'am, I'm happy to put them away for you."

"Good. When you're finished with that, maybe you can help me with making the schedule for the children's story hour. I need help choosing which books will be read next month."

"Sure, Miss Evelyn, I'll be right back." Olivia took off her coat and hung it on the back of a chair, happy to have a purpose, at least for the day.

Miss Evelyn smiled, wondering how long it would take Olivia to catch on. She might have to leave a printout for the librarian certification course hanging around for Olivia to find.

—∞—

Daniel was in his garden shed slash art studio, just finishing the final charcoal sketch. He'd been working on about one per month since he'd arrived, and had almost a dozen now. He was ready for an impromptu art show.

"Good morning, Miss Dot," he said after she picked up the phone. "Is the reverend available?"

"He's with a parishioner right now, Daniel. May I take a message?"

"Sure, I was just wondering if I could use the reception hall for a small art show. I've finished a series of sketches and I'd like to display them, maybe have a little wine and cheese or something."

"That sounds exciting. I'll give the message to Reverend Turner as soon as he's free."

"Thanks, Miss Dot. I hope you can make it too."

"I thank you for the invitation Daniel. Bye for now." She hung up with a smile. She didn't get invited places very often, being the "church lady." This really was exciting!

—◊—

Although everyone was pretty busy leading up to the holiday, Miss Dot found time on the Thursday before Christmas for Daniel to have his art show. Simple posters were put up around town and select locals were asked to attend by special invitation.

Miss Evelyn received her printed invitation and was pleased to RSVP that she would be happy to attend. It was early enough in the evening that she could still get to sleep at a decent hour.

Mr. Gus received his invitation too. He stuck it in the pocket of his overalls with a mental note to get a haircut first. He'd even dig the oil out from under his nails for this shindig.

Ms. Pat read her invitation with a smile on her face and put it in her apron pocket. She planned to get a bit gussied up for this event. And she wouldn't even have to serve the food or drinks.

Daniel kept Emma in the dark about the artwork. He would go to the church personally and mount everything on the walls and partitions, making a walking exhibit so people could go through and come to the final piece at the end.

He was a bit nervous, and appreciated Izzy's prior efforts to display his work. He hadn't heard from her for a while now, and assumed all was well. As they say, no news is good news.

Tracy helped with the wine and cheese trays. Nothing fancy, just things that tasted good together.

Jack set up tables for the food at the entrance to the art show and manned them wearing a dark suit, looking more like Secret Service now than a soldier just rolling in from the desert.

Daniel stood with Emma just inside the doors. She could sense his nervousness and held his hand, squeezing it tightly. "Good luck," she said. "Not that you'll need it."

He smiled in return and let his breath out slowly. They heard voices coming down the hall. "Here we go."

The reverend opened the doors and the guests entered the reception hall, looking around expectantly. Most had never been to an art show before and didn't quite know what to expect.

Daniel stepped forward. "Welcome, everyone. I'm so glad you could make it. I'd like to show you some things I've been working on since I came to Graceville."

"Many of you know me as that guest who came and never left," he joked. The group in attendance laughed.

"When I came to Graceville, I was in a bit of a dark valley. I'd gone through some things, as they say. I'm calling it my charcoal period. But meeting you all, and the Turners... and especially one Turner in particular..."

Emma, standing nearby, blushed as he looked at her and smiled.

"Meeting all of you allowed me to do something I wasn't sure I could do anymore – make art."

He started walking toward the artwork display. "My first inspiration came from a lovely lady with bright-blue eyes who made quite an impression on me." He stopped in front of a charcoal sketch. "Miss Evelyn Miller."

"What? Me?" she exclaimed as the crowd parted to make way for her to stand next to her portrait. Olivia stepped forward to take a picture of the artist on one side of the sketch and the subject on the other. It was a very good likeness. Mild applause ensued and Miss Evelyn looked ready to burst with joy. Daniel leaned down and gave her a kiss on the cheek and her bright-blue eyes brimmed with tears.

"Next we have someone who serves up more than coffee. I was given some very good advice sitting in the Main Street Diner, and Ms. Pat was the inspiration for this next piece."

Once again the crowd made way for the subject to stand next to the artwork and the artist, and Olivia stepped forward to take the picture.

This went on for Ms. Dot, Mr. Gus, Liam, Jack, Tracy, Olivia, and the reverend. There was a sketch of the inn, one of downtown. The attendees all made their way through the show with admiration that this young man, actually quite a renowned artist, had featured them and their town in this way.

As they reached the end, there was one canvas on an easel that was covered with a sheet.

"Once I made it through my charcoal period, things – life – became more colorful for me. With the reverend's help, I started reading the Bible again. I started praying again.

"At first, I didn't even know what to pray for. Just to be free of confusion, mostly. But as time went on, I realized my unspoken prayers were being answered. God knew the prayers of my heart and answered them without my even asking.

"Those answered prayers look something like this."

He gently took a corner of the sheet and lifted it back, to oohs and aahs from the crowd.

There, center stage, was an oil portrait of Emma, sitting on the porch swing of the inn with greenery and colorful flowers behind her. She was wearing a coral-colored sleeveless top and white capris, her legs tucked up under her. He had painted her in vibrant colors, a serene look on her face as she gazed at him from the canvas, her hands resting on a pillow on her lap.

Emma was speechless, gazing at the painting in awe. He had painted her hands to look smooth and strong, just like his own. She looked at her hands now and he took them in his. She gazed up at him in wonderment. Just who was this man who had won her heart?

"Emma, I'm just a man who loves you very much."

There he goes, using the same words again, she thought.

"You helped bring me out of a dark valley onto a hilltop. Your light shines through in everything you do. Emma, you inspire me."

He kissed her on the cheek and Olivia came up to take their picture, barely able to contain her happiness for her sister. She knew that as soon as the crowd left, he'd get down on one knee and propose.

And that's just what he did.

—☙—

Later that night, after all the celebrations had ended, Tracy and Jack were up in their loft apartment. Harvey Sheffield had done a wonderful job fixing it up, leaving most of the original woodwork intact. They had built-in shelves and beautiful wainscoting in the bathroom.

"There's still a draft in here though, even after Harvey added insulation," Jack noted.

"Well, the building is over a hundred years old, isn't it?" countered Tracy. She was tired and happy, and wanted to end the evening on a positive note.

"Yes, but something's telling me to pull these drawers out and check behind them," Jack said. "It'll only take a second." He smiled at his wife, letting her know everything was okay.

He pulled out the top drawer, then the middle, then the bottom drawer. He used a small flashlight to look in the back of the empty space. It all looked tight as a drum. The insulation was not disturbed, and he could no longer feel the draft.

"That is so weird. How can a draft plug itself up?" he muttered as he began putting the drawers back in. He picked one up by the hand and stood up to swing it into place.

"Jack, wait, there's something stuck to the bottom of the drawer," said Tracy as she stood in the doorway.

Jack paused and looked down. Sure enough, there was an envelope stuck into the corner of the drawer.

"What the...?" Jack said as he inspected the envelope more closely. "To The One True God," he read. He took the envelope off the drawer and put the drawer down. He turned the envelope over a number of times, then placed his finger under the seal.

"Wait. Should we open it?" Tracy asked.

"Sure, why not?"

"Because it belongs to the family."

"Well, it's too late to show them now. I'll give it to them in the morning, but I won't sleep a wink until I open it. It's not like it's addressed to them. It's addressed to God."

"All right," Tracy said a bit doubtfully.

Jack carefully opened the envelope and took out the aged piece of paper with expressive writing on it. "Uh-oh, it's written in cursive. They stopped teaching that in school when I was about ten years old." He squinted at the page, moving it forward and backward to try to make sense of it.

"For you... so... something the something..." He scanned the rest of the letter. "Oh, so loved the world, you gave your only Son that whoever believes in him shall not perish but shall have eternal life. John 3:16."

He looked at Tracy.

"That's really nice," she said. "Kind of like a blessing on the house."

"Yeah, maybe we should just put it back and not say anything."

"Good idea."

Jack put the letter back, inserted the drawers, and they went to sleep a little easier knowing God was watching over them.

Printed in the United States
by Baker & Taylor Publisher Services